W9-BNS-962

Hands shaking, Mia sprayed the water vigorously, but there was simply not enough flow to combat the hungry fire.

She retreated to the front porch, skin stinging from the poisonous air.

Dallas appeared at the upstairs window. He shouted something to Mia, but she could not understand. The fire was nearly upon her, heat scalded her face and hands, smoke filling her lungs. She backed farther away, praying the fire engine would arrive soon to douse the flames.

Finally, Dallas came out carrying Cora and led her away from the burning house.

Mia put her mouth to the woman's cheek, praying for a reassuring puff of air. Panic swirled through her veins as she felt nothing at all. Starting CPR, she pressed her hands to Cora's chest.

"Come on, Cora," she said. "You're not going to leave me now."

Dallas dropped to his knees and performed the rescue breaths at the end of her compression cycles. After a full minute, Dallas checked her pulse.

He shook his head.

Tears trickled down Mia's cheeks as she began the next cycle.

Books by Dana Mentink

Love Inspired Suspense

DANA MENTINK

is an award-winning author of Christian fiction. Her novel *Betrayal in the Badlands* won a 2010 RT Reviewer's Choice Award, and she was pleased to win the 2013 Carol Award for *Lost Legacy*. She has authored more than a dozen Love Inspired Suspense novels. Dana loves feedback from her readers. Contact her via her website at www.danamentink.com.

FLOOD ZONE
DANA MENTINK

⟨H⟩ **HARLEQUIN**® LOVE INSPIRED® SUSPENSE

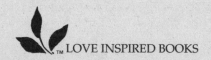 LOVE INSPIRED BOOKS

Recycling programs for this product may not exist in your area.

ISBN-13: 978-0-373-44608-7

FLOOD ZONE

Trust in the Lord with all your heart;
do not depend on your own understanding.
Seek his will in all you do,
and he will show you which path to take.
—*Proverbs* 3:5–6

To my Mike,
who is always there through the floods.

ONE

Forget meeting tonight. Must speak to you and Dallas now. URGENT.

Mia risked another peek at the cell phone screen as she guided her battered Toyota up the steep mountain grade to Cora's country house just after six in the evening. She'd thought Cora's proposed after-hours meeting at the medical clinic where they both worked was odd in the first place. Now the message to cancel. Stranger still. But Cora had been acting oddly, excusing herself to take phone calls, peeping into file folders squirreled away in her desk for weeks. On this particular day, Cora had left at lunch time. Strange.

Her gaze darted to the rearview mirror. Dallas Black drove his truck behind her. Something about the tall, tousle-headed rebel made her stomach flip, no matter how sternly she chided herself.

Look what the last dark-eyed charmer did to you, Mia.

Stuffing that uncomfortable thought back down into the secret place where she kept all her worries, Mia focused on navigating the winding, wet road, finally pulling onto Cora's graveled drive. Dallas got out, long and lean in jeans and a T-shirt, a couple of months overdue for a haircut. Somehow, the hair spidering across his face suited him, refusing to play nicely.

ONE

Forget meeting tonight. Must speak to you and Dallas now. URGENT.

Mia risked another peek at the cell phone screen as she guided her battered Toyota up the steep mountain grade to Cora's country house just after six in the evening. She'd thought Cora's proposed after-hours meeting at the medical clinic where they both worked was odd in the first place. Now the message to cancel. Stranger still. But Cora had been acting oddly, excusing herself to take phone calls, peeping into file folders squirreled away in her desk for weeks. On this particular day, Cora had left at lunch time. Strange.

Her gaze darted to the rearview mirror. Dallas Black drove his truck behind her. Something about the tall, tousle-headed rebel made her stomach flip, no matter how sternly she chided herself.

Look what the last dark-eyed charmer did to you, Mia.

Stuffing that uncomfortable thought back down into the secret place where she kept all her worries, Mia focused on navigating the winding, wet road, finally pulling onto Cora's graveled drive. Dallas got out, long and lean in jeans and a T-shirt, a couple of months overdue for a haircut. Somehow, the hair spidering across his face suited him, refusing to play nicely.

Dallas sprinted up the drive with Mia right behind him. They cleared the thickly clustered cottonwood trees in time to hear the whoosh of breaking glass when the lower story window exploded. Mia nearly skidded into him as the shards rained down on the muddy ground.

Her mind struggled to process what was happening. He gripped her arms, and she saw the tiny reflected flames burning in his chocolate irises. "Call for help. Keep Juno out."

Mia's hands shook so badly she could barely manage to hold on to both the phone and Juno's collar. The dog was barking furiously, yanking against her restraining arm in an effort to get to his owner. Nearly eighty pounds of muscle, Juno was determined, and he definitely did not see her as the boss.

Frantically, she dialed the emergency number. Tears started in her eyes as she realized she was not getting a signal. The tall Colorado mountain peaks in the distance interfered. She would have to move and see if she could find another spot that would work. Dragging Juno with one hand, she made her way back toward the car. They'd only gotten about ten feet when Juno broke loose from her grasp and ran straight for the burning house.

"Juno, stop!" she yelled. The smoke was now roiling through the downstairs, and she'd lost sight of Dallas. There was no choice but to keep trying to find a place to make the call. Three times she tried before she got a signal.

"Please help," she rasped. "Cora Graham's house on Stick Pine Road is on fire."

The dispatcher gave her a fifteen minute ETA.

Her heart sank. They could both be dead in fifteen minutes. She stowed the phone in her pocket and ran to the front porch where she remembered there was a hose Cora used to water her patches of brilliant snapdragons. The wood of the old house crackled violently, letting loose with a spark every now and then that burned little holes through the fabric of her jacket. One started to smolder, and she slapped a hand to snuff it out. Flames flashed out the first-floor windows. Juno barked furiously, dashing in helpless fits and starts, unsure how to get to his master.

She cranked the hose and squirted the water at the open front door. *Where are you, Dallas?* Inside, the flames had spread through the sitting room, enveloping the oak furniture in crackling orange and yellow. She climbed up the porch steps, dousing the wood with water and forcing her way into the entry, past the spurts of flame.

She sprayed the water vigorously, but there was simply not enough flow to combat the hungry fire. She retreated to the front porch, skin stinging from the poisonous air.

Dallas appeared at the upstairs window. He shouted something to Mia, but she could not understand. The fire was nearly upon her, heat scalded her face and hands, smoke filling her lungs. She backed farther away, praying the fire engine would arrive soon to douse the flames.

There was no welcoming wail of sirens.

She scanned the upper story and once again caught sight of Dallas. He was batting at the flaming curtains with a blanket. She saw a way she could help. Climbing a few feet up an ivy-covered trellis allowed her to stretch the hose far enough that she could train the water on the burning fabric. Dallas jerked in surprise and then disappeared back inside, returning a moment later with Cora in his arms and stepping onto the roof. Mia's heart lodged in her throat as she watched Dallas walking on the precariously pitched shingles with his precious burden.

His feet skidded, and he fell on his back, somehow stopping his slide before he fell over the edge. Mia jumped off the trellis and cast the hose aside. "Here, lower her down to me."

It was an awkward process, but Dallas managed to ease

Cora low enough that Mia could grab her around the waist. Staggering under the weight, she tottered backwards until Dallas jumped down and they both carried Cora away from the burning house. Juno raced behind them to a flat spot of grass where they laid the old woman. Dallas ordered the dog to stay.

Mia brushed sooty hair away from Cora's forehead. Her sparkling blue eyes were closed, her mouth, slack. She put her cheek to Cora's mouth, praying for a reassuring puff of air. Panic swirled through her veins as she felt nothing at all. Starting CPR, she pressed her hands to Cora's chest.

"Come on, Cora," she said. "You're not going to leave me now."

Dallas dropped to his knees and performed the rescue breaths at the end of her compression cycles. After a full minute, Dallas checked her pulse.

He shook his head.

Tears trickled down Mia's cheeks as she began the next cycle. "You haven't finished learning Italian," she said to Cora. "You're only on lesson three, and that's not going to be enough if you want to go to Rome." Another set of compressions and rescue breaths.

This time she didn't allow herself to look at Dallas. Cora was going to live. Shoulders aching she pressed with renewed vigor. "And your nephew is happily married in Seattle. He's not going to want to come and take care of this sprawling old place, isn't that what you always said, Cora?"

Sirens pierced the air and a fire truck appeared through the smoke, rumbling up the grade, followed by an ambulance. Mia did not slow her efforts.

"You wake up right now, do you hear me? I mean it. I told you over and over not to keep those silly scented candles in your bedroom. They did not keep away the mosquitos, no matter what you say. You wake up so I can chew you out properly." Tears dripped from her face and cleared spots of black from Cora's forehead.

The medics ran over, but stopped short when Juno barked at them until Dallas quieted him. They pushed forward, eyeing the big dog suspiciously, and edged Mia out of the way.

"I have to stay with her," she pleaded.

Dallas drew her back, his voice oddly soft. "They've got it, Mia. Let them work."

"But…"

He gently, but firmly, took her arm and moved her several yards distant from the paramedics.

She breathed in and out, forcing herself to stop crying. "I'm okay, I'm okay," she repeated, waving him away when he came close.

Dallas stood there, long muscled arms black with soot, the edges of his hair singed at the tips, looking at her until she couldn't stand it anymore. "What is it? What are you thinking?"

Dallas didn't answer.

"Please tell me." She moved closer, the dark pools of his eyes not giving away anything.

Dallas considered. "I wasn't sure what type of service dog Juno would be. Before I trained him in Search and Rescue, a buddy of mine had a go at making him a drug-sniffing dog, but Juno doesn't obey anyone but me, so he flunked out. Mastered only the first lesson."

"What are you saying?"

He pulled a plastic pill bottle from his pocket. "These were on the bedside table. Do you know what she takes them for?"

Mia took the bottle and held it up to the light from the engines. "It's her blood pressure medication. I pick up her prescriptions myself."

Dallas frowned.

Mia felt the seeds of dread take hold deep down. She put her hands on Dallas's unyielding chest. "Dallas, please tell me what you're thinking."

"The first lesson, the only one that Juno mastered..."

She found she was holding her breath as he finished.

"Was alerting on drugs...like cocaine."

Dallas mentally berated himself for mentioning Juno's behavior at that moment. Mia was already trembling as the shock of what had happened settled in.

Should've waited. How many times had he said that to himself?

This time he did not allow her to pull away when he folded her in a smoky embrace. She was so small, so slight in his arms, and he resisted the urge to run his hands along her shoulders. He thought of all the things he should say, the comforts he could whisper in her ear, but everything fled, driven away by the feel of her. She stiffened suddenly, and he wondered if she'd been hurt in the fire.

"There," Mia gasped, pointing behind the house.

He turned in time to see a woman with a wild tangle of red hair framed by the trees that backed the property. She stood frozen for a moment, eyes wide and face soot-stained and then she bolted into the woods.

"Stop," Dallas called, and he and Juno took off into the trees, Mia stumbling along behind.

"Who was that?" she asked, panting.

He didn't know.

"I thought I saw her outside the clinic one time, talking to Cora, but I'm not sure," Mia said.

A cursory search yielded nothing, though the falling rain and smoke didn't help. After a short time, they left off looking to follow the ambulance to the hospital.

In the waiting room, Mia sat on a hard-backed chair, and Dallas paced as much as the narrow hallway would allow until the doctor delivered his news. "I'm sorry. She didn't make it."

Dallas watched the spirit leak out of Mia as she put her head in her hands. Something cut at him, something deeper than the grief at Cora's death. He swallowed hard and stepped aside with the doctor. "Do you have a cause of death?"

The physician, whose name tag read Dr. Carp, hesitated. "She was dead upon arrival, but we called the police immediately after you told us about the pills. They took possession of them. Autopsy will be later this week." That much Dallas already knew as he and Mia had told their story to a young uniformed cop named Brownley.

The doctor left and Dallas sat next to Mia. He didn't speak. There was nothing to say anyway. Best to wait until she could articulate the thoughts that rolled across her face like wind sweeping through grass. Finally, he took her hand, hoping she would not yank it away. She didn't.

"Cora wanted to tell us something, something important," Mia said, her voice wobbling as she clutched his fingers. "Can you guess anything at all about what it was?"

Dallas shook his head. "No."

"I'm sure Juno was wrong about the pills," she said, a tiny pleading note to her voice. "Those were for her blood pressure. I delivered them to her myself. They couldn't have hurt her. Could they?"

He covered her hand with his palm. "Whatever this is, however it went down, was not your fault."

"That woman… Who was she?" Her brown eyes were haunted. "Dallas…" she whispered. "I'm scared."

He pulled her to her feet then and embraced her because he did not know the words to say. He never did, probably never would. "I'm taking you home."

A short, balding man with a thick, silvered mustache

came close. "In a minute. I'm Detective Stiving, Ms. Verde, and I need to ask you some questions."

Dallas felt his gut tighten. Stiving. Perfect.

He and Stiving had been oil and water since Dallas had butted in on a missing-person's case and found a teen lost near Rockglen Creek whom Stiving had insisted was a runaway.

"Kid's a loose cannon," Stiving had insisted. "Drinks and parties like his father."

Runaway or lost, Dallas and Juno found the kid named Farley who'd fallen into a ravine, and the press was there to catch it. Since then, Dallas had gotten a bogus speeding ticket and been stopped twice by Stiving for no particular reason. Not good, but in a small town like Spanish Canyon, Stiving was it.

"Doc says you're making allegations about drugs," Stiving said, holding up the bottle of pills nestled in an evidence bag. "Looking to get some more publicity for yourself?"

"Juno alerted on that pill bottle."

"Juno is a drug-sniffing flunk-out, from what I've heard. I thought his forte was tracking down idiots who get lost in the woods."

Mia wiped her sleeve across her cheeks. "What kind of talk is that for a law enforcement officer?" she said indignantly. "Cora is…was a long-time resident of this town. I should think you'd want to be thorough investigating her death."

His blue eyes narrowed, face blotching with color. "Yes, Ms. Verde, I will. I started by running a check on you. It made for interesting reading. Since you've had such a long and storied history with law enforcement, I guess you'd know that I'll be contacting you for follow up information as soon as I get this to the lab."

Mia went white and then red.

Dallas clenched his jaw. *Don't mouth off to the cops, Dallas.* "We saw a woman with red hair running away from the house."

Stiving blinked. "Really? Did you recognize her?"

Mia shook her head. "She might have come to the clinic to talk to Cora, but I'm not sure. I only saw her for a moment."

"And you?"

Dallas shrugged.

"Right. Well, we'll investigate that while we're checking into things." The detective's phone rang, and he walked away to answer it and then left abruptly.

Mia put a hand on Dallas's wrist, her fingers ice cold. "I have to go. Tina needs to get home, and I want to read Gracie a story before bed." She looked at her soiled clothes. "It will take some explaining about why I look like this." Her lip trembled. "I'll need to tell Gracie about Cora."

He wondered how a woman with filthy hair, torn clothes and a grief-stained face could look so beautiful, like Whistler's painting of the woman in white he'd seen in his mother's art books decades ago. Would she be so trusting if she knew the truth about what brought him to town? Dallas had been many things in his life, a gang member, a wanderer and a drinker. He'd never been a liar, not until now, with her. It tightened something deep in his gut. He had to remind himself he had good reasons for the subterfuge.

He'd been hired by Antonia, Mia's sister, to keep watch over her due to the prevalence of Mia's ex-husband Hector Sandoval's many enemies. Cora, a friend of Antonia's new husband, was in on the whole thing. An accomplice, he thought ruefully, who'd arranged for Dallas to hang out on her property just as often as the stubborn and ferociously independent Mia did.

He returned to the truck where Juno was sound asleep and waited until Mia got into her car. Following her home, he ran things over in his mind. Cora was obviously disturbed when she messaged both Dallas and Mia. How coincidental was it that her house burned down and she lost her life on the very same night Mia spotted some mystery woman fleeing the scene? Very coincidental, and Dallas Black did not believe in coincidence any more than he believed that Elvis still strolled planet Earth.

He walked Mia to her front door and waited while she stepped into the tiny front room.

Four-year-old Gracie came flying down the hall, short bob of hair bouncing around her, eyes alight with pleasure at the sight of him. They'd encountered each other many times at Cora's house while he was on the roof and she was digging holes around the property. When rain interrupted the roofing, they built card houses together, impressed with their creations until Juno knocked them over with a jerk of his tail.

"Did you come to play?" She took in his appearance and laughed. "You need a shower, Mr. Dallas."

He laughed, too, and Mia tried to draw Gracie away.

"Can he come in for a snack?" the child asked. "I've got Goldfish."

Dallas got down on one knee. "You eat goldfish? Don't the fins get stuck in your teeth?"

She giggled. "They're cracker fish. Juno will like them."

"Juno can't have Goldfish tonight, but we'll come another time."

She frowned. "Okay, but what if I don't have Goldfish then? Mommy eats them sometimes when I'm asleep and she's off her diet."

Mia's face flushed, and Dallas hid a grin.

"Tell you what, Goldfish girl. Next time I come with Juno, I'll bring some Goldfish along. How's that?"

She nodded, finally trotting off into the kitchen.

"You don't have to make good on that promise," Mia

whispered as she let Dallas out. "As a matter of fact, I'd rather you didn't promise her things at all. I know you'd never mean to disappoint, but Gracie's been let down in a big way by her father."

"No sweat," he said. Something flickered in her face, something thoughtful. "You're not planning to go to the clinic, right?"

Mia jerked. "How did you know I was thinking about that?"

"Call it a knack. Don't go there by yourself, just in case whatever she was looking into has something to do with the fire."

She stayed silent.

"If you do have to go, I'll go with you."

She offered a courteous smile. "Thanks, Dallas. I appreciate it."

But you'll never allow it. He understood. He recognized the shadows that danced in her eyes for what they were. Fear. A desperate, ponderous weight of fear that she did not want to expose to anyone. Who would? He'd known that, tasted that when he was being beaten within an inch of his life during his gang days. That fear was hideous and bred on itself, multiplying exponentially the longer it was kept in the dark, like a poisonous fungus. He wished he could tell her. There is only one antidote, One who could defeat that fear. Instead, he remained silent until he heard the sound of the lock turning.

Juno and Dallas made one more stop on the way home, purchasing a bone for Juno and a handful of hot peppers for himself. With some help from the store clerk, he also secured five bags of Goldfish crackers, which he stowed in the back of his truck. Who knew Goldfish came in so many flavors? Dallas smiled to himself. Gracie knew, and that was enough.

TWO

The parking lot was empty, quiet, save for the patter of a cold rain and the scuff of Mia's shoes as she made her way to the darkened clinic hours later. She was grateful that Tina offered to stay late. It was almost eight by the time Mia embarked on her mission. She knew she should have called Dallas, but the only thing that scared her more than what had happened to Cora was the thought of losing herself to another man who would betray her and Gracie. She realized her hands were in her pockets, hidden away, a habit she'd developed after she'd stabbed her husband.

The horror lapped at her afresh. Her own hands had lashed out with that knife, powered by terror that Hector would kill her and take Gracie away into his corrupt world. She would never have done it, but she believed, heart and soul, that Hector meant to end her life. After Mia's arrest, she'd endured six months of jail time, knowing Gracie was with Hector, near people both ruthless and greed-driven, the worst being her own husband. After her release, she'd fled with Gracie, unaware that Hector would soon concoct a plot to outwit his enemies that involved kidnapping her sister, Antonia. While her sister fought for her life on a hurricane-ravaged island, Mia hid out like a frightened rabbit.

Sometimes her mind told her it was a dream, a nightmare, but she still remembered the feel of that knife in her hand and how her life had almost ended because she trusted the wrong man in spite of her father's warnings, Antonia's pleadings. In spite of her own troubled intuition.

Never again. Better to go it alone. A quick stop at the clinic. See if by chance Cora had left anything there that might be of help. In and out. Something wheeled along by her feet, and she gasped. Just a leaf, torn loose by the storm.

She bit back a wave of self-disgust at finding herself scuttling along, cringing at every leaf. She was an office clerk at the Spanish Canyon Clinic after all, and Cora was, had been, a volunteer. All perfectly aboveboard. But why had Cora originally insisted they wait until long after closing time to meet?

Her throat ached when she thought of her friend. Had she suffered? Had she known her house was burning around her?

Quickening her pace she sought shelter from the spring rain under the awning, keys ready in her hand, heart beating a little too hard, too erratically. Cora's nightmarish death came on a date that already held terrible memories, her wedding anniversary.

An annual reminder of the worst mistake of her life. But Hector had been so gentle when they'd first met, even professing to be a Christian, until he'd begun to worship another kind of God, the god of money, power and excitement, when he'd gotten involved in the drug trade. It was long over. Hector was jailed on new charges, the divorce finalized two years before, but Hector did not want to accept his losses, so she lived as anonymous a life as she could manage.

With teeth gritted, she wondered—Had Hector found her again?

His reach hadn't extended to Spanish Canyon, Colorado. Not this time.

Wind carried a cold spray of rain onto her face that trickled down the back of her neck. She wished there was someone else around, the janitor, a late working nurse, anyone. They might be parked in the underground garage, she thought hopefully. With a surge of relief she saw the lights on in the back of the building where she and Cora shared a desk.

Jamming her key in the lock, she left the rain behind and headed down the silent corridor to the rear of the building. She did not know what she hoped to accomplish. Maybe it was all just a way to keep busy.

Cora's desk was bare, save for a paperweight rock engraved with the words *Be Still*. An impossible task, it seemed, for the nearly eighty-year-old woman who had recently decided to learn Italian and tour Europe. Her eyes were drawn to her own desk. Shadows must be deceiving. Silhouetted in the lamplight was a vase full of long-stemmed roses. Trancelike, she moved closer and turned on her own work light. Yellow roses, which had once been her favorite. A gilt-edged card.

I'm sorry. I love you and we can be a family again. Hector.

Sweat beaded on her forehead. It was as if he was there, right there, standing in the shadows. Fear turned into hatred for the man who had stripped away her belief in herself.

Hector didn't strip it away. You handed it over, wrapped in a bow.

The floor creaked, and she spun around with a scream.

"I'm sorry," Dr. Elias said with an apologetic smile. "I didn't mean to scare you. I was working late and noticed the florist had been here. Nice roses. Curiosity won out, and I checked the card." He raised an apologetic eyebrow, the fiftysomething face calm and serene. "My wife says I'm incurably nosey, and I hate to admit that she's got me pegged."

Mia forced out a calming breath. "I'm surprised to see you here so late."

"Insomnia. It usually sends me to the computer to play solitaire, but I get tired of beating myself, so I come here sometimes."

"Did you…did you hear about Cora?"

He nodded, mournfully. "Tragic. Cora was an excellent lady and a noble spirit." He shook his head. "Why do the good die before their time?"

It was a question she'd asked many times to a God who'd never given her a straight answer.

Dr. Elias cleared his throat. "Anyway, I'm glad you came so you could get your flowers, but why so late? Insomnia trouble for you also?"

She was about to tell him about the prearranged meeting with Cora, but something stopped her. "I just wanted to clean up Cora's desk."

"Looks clean already." Something in his inflection made her wonder if he'd been looking through Cora's belongings. Ridiculous. Crazy suspicion.

He surveyed the ceiling for a long moment. "It's good, actually, that we have a private moment so we can talk. I feel as though I have treated you well, hired you on in spite of your criminal record."

She winced. "Yes, you have. I appreciate that."

"It was Cora who went to bat for you, you know. She felt passionately that you would be an asset to this clinic. I was reluctant, I'll admit."

Mia started. She hadn't even known Cora when she moved to Spanish Canyon. She'd been following a lead on a job that her sister had dug up. Close to nursing school. Quiet town where nobody knew her.

"So I'm loathe to ask it, Mia, but when were you going to mention the truth about your criminal husband?"

She kept her chin high, even though at five three she barely reached his shoulder. Her phone vibrated in her pocket. "Ex-husband."

He blinked, his smooth complexion bordered by a distinguished head of gray hair that went well with his stature as head of the town's largest general medicine clinic. "I knew he was abusive, you were arrested for stabbing him I realize, but you didn't quite tell me the whole story. The flowers got me curious and I did a little checking. Nosey, just like my wife says. He wasn't just an abusive spouse. He's a Miami drug kingpin with powerful friends." His pale gray eyes locked on hers. "You didn't feel like you should mention that?"

Mention it? She was too busy trying to forget it.

"Is that why you don't use your married name? Sandoval?"

"It's not my name because I'm not married anymore. I haven't been for years. Simple as that."

He looked at the ceiling again while he talked. "Not really so simple. I've tried to support you here, to give you the hours you need to get you through nursing school and help you earn some money to keep food on the table for Gracie."

She didn't like it when he said Gracie's name, for some reason that she could not articulate. Did she feel the swell of distrust when she looked at him because he had the same self-assured manner as Hector? The doctor had been nothing but gracious.

"I would do anything for my own kids, as you know. It hasn't always been easy to afford everything times two, but that's the price of having twins. Jake and Renee are both in private high school now, so I understand wanting the best for your kids. But why lie? Especially to me."

"I never lied. You asked about my ex-husband, and I told you the reason I was sent to jail."

"You neglected to mention your husband is a Miami drug lord. You thought you'd pulled the wool over my eyes, didn't you? Simple country doctor. Easy to do, you figured?"

"No, nothing like that, really," she said.

The phone buzzed again.

Something sparked in his eyes. "Omissions are lies, and I'm afraid I'm going to have to ask you to leave." His brow furrowed. "It pains me to do it, it really does, but I have a professional obligation, no matter what my personal feelings are. My patients have to have absolute trust in me and my staff, and if you're still getting flowers from a drug kingpin, I can't risk having you here."

Mia would not let him see her cry. Head high, she nodded. "I'll be out of here in fifteen minutes." She went to the desk in the corner of the Spanish Canyon Clinic and shoved the picture of Gracie into a bag along with a collection of notepads. Cora's *Learn Italian Today* book was on her desk, under a box of tissue, and she scooped it up as well. She'd never dropped a phone call, never misplaced a file or been anything but pleasant to everyone and even that wasn't enough to overshadow her disastrous marriage.

Blinking to keep the tears at bay, her mind ran wild. No job. How would she finish school? Would it be the end of her dreams to finally give Gracie a stable, normal life? Her phone demanded her attention again and this time she yanked it from her pocket. It was a text from Dallas.

Ok?

Was she?

Dr. Elias still stood there, filling the doorway with his

blocky shoulders, a look of indecision on his face. "This husband, Hector. He's tracked you everywhere, hasn't he?"

One of the notepads sliced into her finger giving her a paper cut. She shook off the sting angrily.

"Hector must be jealous." The lamplight etched Dr. Elias in tight shadow. "Have you given him reason?"

She froze. "What?"

"The tough guy with the dog. I've seen him talking to you. Hector can't be happy about this."

Seen Dallas? Something cold trickled through her. Why had Dr. Elias noticed whom she'd been talking to?

He flicked a glance into her bag. "You're not taking any clinic information, are you?"

She burned. "No, Doctor. I would not behave unethically, even after I've been wrongly terminated."

A glimmer of a smile lit his face. "I always liked your spunk, Mia Verde Sandoval. Too bad."

Mia grabbed her bag and purse and went to the door, but he barred her path.

He didn't move, just watched her as if he was weighing something in his mind. He reached out a hand to touch her forearm, but she recoiled.

"Hold on. I can see the truth now. You didn't lie to deceive, you lied because you're afraid."

Her breath caught and she shook her head.

"Yes, that's it, isn't it? You're afraid that Hector will find you." He stared closely at her. "No, you're afraid that you can't trust yourself, your choices, your judgments." He took her arm.

The fingers felt cold there against her skin, her own feet rooted to the floor. It was as if he'd stepped inside her, peered into the cold dark place in her heart where she herself dared not go.

"I know what it's like to be lied to. I'm so sorry, Mia," he said, pupils glittering in the dimly lit office. He leaned toward her and lowered his voice to a whisper. "I'm dense, sometimes. I didn't realize. I can help you."

Standing this close she realized how strong he looked. Her fingers clutched her car keys, and she raised them in front of her.

"I want to leave. Now."

He laughed and moved a step closer. She was acutely aware of how empty the clinic was, how dark the outer corridors. "You're a beautiful woman, you know that?" His gaze flickered up and down her body. "You deserve more. I can help you get your life back."

She pressed back until she bumped into the file cabinets, a metal handle digging into her spine. He put his hands out, kneading her shoulders.

She jerked away from his grasp. "I want to go," she whispered, gripping the keys. "I will scream the place down if you touch me again."

He chuckled. "You came here after hours, almost as if you were looking for me."

The implication was clear. *Who do you think they'll believe?*

She gripped the keys, palms clammy, readying herself to gouge and bite and kick. Unsure.

"You're not seeing things clearly, Mia. You don't know what's right and wrong anymore, do you?" The words were almost a whisper, his mouth curved in a soft smile. "You need help."

Help? Was that what he offered? Her gut told her to run. Should she trust that instinct?

From somewhere far away, she heard herself say, "I want to go. Now."

"Maybe you don't know what you want," he said, eyes glittering.

"Yes, she does," said a low voice. The doctor was jerked back and dumped in an unceremonious pile on the floor.

Dallas Black looked down at Elias, his dark eyes blending with the shadows.

She realized Dallas must have been expecting her to act stupidly and visit the clinic and her cheeks burned, but relief overrode any other sensation.

"I was just fired," Mia announced. "And now I'm going to leave."

Dallas didn't move. "Good. Doesn't pay to work for dirtbags."

"Trespassing and assault," Dr. Elias snapped at Dallas, scrambling to his feet. "I will have you arrested."

Dallas ignored the comment completely. "Ready to go?" he said to her.

"Get off my property," Dr. Elias snarled. Gone was the genial smile, any vestiges of warmth, fire blazed in his eyes.

Mia gripped her bag and walked to the door on shaky legs, grateful to have Dallas looking over her shoulder at the doctor. She was desperate to end the situation. Dallas had a complete disregard for rules and she wanted to finish the whole confrontation before anything worse happened.

"You are turning away from someone who wants to help you, Mia," Dr. Elias said, nostrils flared. "And look what you're walking into."

"Goodbye, Dr. Elias," Mia said.

"Don't forget your flowers," he yelled.

"Keep them," she said.

Dallas's truck was parked at the curb, and Juno sat next to it. When he saw her his tail went into overtime, and he whined until she gave him a cursory pat. He licked her face.

"If a man approached my ride, Juno would bark up a storm, but with you he'd hand over the keys," Dallas said. *Smart dog.*

Juno was once an aggressive shelter resident after having been beaten and starved by a cruel owner. Dallas had spent six months tracking down that negligent owner on his own dime, until the man was charged with animal cruelty and subjected to hefty fines. It wasn't enough in Dallas's view.

Mia straightened in spite of Juno's disappointment and gave him a tight smile. "He must know I'm a cat person and he's trying to help me see the light." She paused. "I would have handled the situation, you know. No one will keep me from Gracie."

"No doubt. I'm just glad I was in the neighborhood." In truth he'd been driving around town, too restless to stay home, checking the clinic lot every so often in case Mia showed up like he suspected she'd do. "I'm not sure..." She bit her lip. "I don't know if Dr. Elias was going to hurt me. He said he wanted to help."

Help? That wasn't what Dallas had heard in the good doctor's tone when he put his hands on Mia. "What did your gut tell you?"

"To leave."

"Then you did the right thing." Dallas clamped down on the anger that ticked at his insides. His own instincts told him Dr. Elias was interested in much more than Mia's well-being. He despised the thought of Elias being anywhere near Mia. Or touching her. Or looking in her general direction.

Overprotective, Black.

Overprotective? How could that be when she kept him at arm's length and he wasn't interested in a relationship anyway? Whatever the reason, something about her, her strength perhaps, stayed in his mind like a lingering fragrance.

It made him pretty sure that if she knew the real reason he'd come to Spanish Canyon, to protect her without her consent, she'd let him have it with both barrels, but the roses on her desk indicated there was ample cause for him to keep an eye on her.

He'd met Mia at the wedding of her sister, Antonia, to Hector's brother Reuben Sandoval after the two barely survived a hurricane. Oddly, he'd befriended Antonia three years prior in the wake of a massive earthquake that struck San Francisco where he assisted his brother, Trey, in rescuing Antonia and Sage Harrington, now Trey's wife. At least Antonia and Trey had both found love matches in the midst of disaster. A memory from that wedding stayed sharp in his mind. Mia's face torn with sorrow, or was it guilt, cradling Gracie in her arms. Hemingway said people healed stronger where they were broken. Mia, though she didn't ever discuss her past, was like that, he figured. *Sometimes it takes more strength to ask for help than to go it alone, Mia.*

He snapped out of his reverie when she sighed heavily. "Go ahead and say it. I was dumb to come here, after hours, in light of all that's happened."

He considered. "Yeah."

"I have good reasons for doing things my own way."

"Don't we all." He tried to catch her eye, but she avoided his gaze. "You okay?"

"Yes."

"Sure?"

"I'm perfectly fine," she said with a little too much bravado. He caught the tremble of her lips in spite of the dim light. It made his stomach tighten.

"I'll follow you home again."

"I'm fine. There's no reason."

"It's dark, weather's bad and you were harassed. That's three reasons." He opened the door for her.

She rolled her eyes and started to get into the car when the bag slipped from her hands. She snatched it up but not before Cora's Italian book plopped out. It fell open, and she saw something stuck inside. Picking it up hastily, she said, "What's this?"

From between the pages she pulled out a four-by-six photo, and Dallas shone his penlight on it.

"We've seen this woman before," she said grimly.

Dallas felt a stir of foreboding flow through his belly. "Running away from Cora's burning house."

THREE

Sleep eluded Mia. Though she felt like throwing herself on the floor and sobbing at the loss of her dear friend, she would not allow Gracie to witness such an outburst. The best thing she could offer now was a heavy dose of mothering in between scouring the want ads and internet sites for employment opportunities. A breakfast of scrambled eggs, toast cut into a heart shape, and a half dozen stories later, and Gracie was content to go into the soggy backyard and hunt for snails. Unless the snails had teeny scuba suits, Mia didn't think she'd have much luck.

She sat on the couch and considered the facts.

The little house they now occupied was rented. Cora had helped her find the place, and though she received a settlement when she divorced Hector, she steadfastly refused to take any child-support money. Dr. Elias was right. Hector Sandoval was involved in the drug trade, and she did not want a single penny of tainted money to find its way to Gracie.

Hector claimed in every letter that he'd repented, but she did not believe him or any other man for that matter. The most important person in her life was Gracie, and Mia would not fail her. So how could she tell her daughter about Cora? Images of the fire raced through her memory, especially the moment when the red-haired woman had appeared through the smoke. Whoever she was, she had answers. Hopefully, the police chief could help ferret out the truth, though he'd not been able to grant her an audience until the following day. Dallas had advised her to bypass Stiving, and she'd agreed. It was best to talk to the chief. For now, the picture was tucked safely in an envelope in the back of the top desk drawer.

The doorbell rang.

Tina stepped inside, chewing madly on a piece of pink gum with a stack of books under her arm to be perused during Gracie's nap time. Mia greeted her warmly. The stick-thin college sophomore babysat for Mia during the day and took community classes at night. Since Mia's nursing school was off due to a semester break, she'd been logging as many hours at Dr. Elias's clinic as she could and Tina had been invaluable. The two exchanged a quiet talk about Cora's death, news of which had already spread all over the quiet mountain community.

"Have you told her yet?" Tina asked, discarding her gum into a wrapper and snatching a leftover piece of toast.

"No." Mia sighed, eyes misting. "I haven't had the courage."

Tina gave her a hug which almost loosed the flood gates of emotion until Mia stepped back. "I'm glad you could come today. I've got to find another job."

"Yeah? What happened to the gig at the clinic?"

"I was…let go last night."

Tina swallowed the last bit of toast. "Oh, bummer. What are you going to do now?"

"Go into town and beat the bushes if I have to. Anything to make the rent."

"That's the spirit."

Mia nodded. "There's got to be somebody looking for a hard-working gal like me."

"We are women, hear us roar," Tina cried, pumping a fist. "Go get 'em!"

Wishing she could share some of Tina's enthusiasm, she grabbed her bag. After they'd made arrangements for Tina to deliver Gracie to Mia in the late afternoon, she headed for the car.

"Time to hit it," she murmured to herself. "Hear me roar."

Fearing that her roar was more like a pitiful mew at the moment, she headed to town.

After a full day of walking the main streets of Spanish Canyon, Mia had nothing to show for it but sore feet and a rumbling belly. She'd already gobbled her peanut butter and marshmallow fluff sandwich, and at a little past three, her stomach was demanding attention, as it seemed to do no matter what diet she was doing her best to adhere to. Besides, a sign on Sam's Sammies advertised for "help wanted."

I'm a master of the peanut butter and fluff, she reminded herself as she entered and introduced herself to the owner.

Sam Shepherd, a massive man with sprigs of white hair sprouting from the top of his head met her inquiry with enthusiasm. "Sure thing. Why don't you fill out an application?" He pushed over a greasy piece of paper affixed to a clipboard. "Say, I was sure sorry to hear about Cora."

She nodded. "Me, too."

"You know her well?"

Mia only managed a quick yes.

He raised a bristly eyebrow. "Heard talk that it wasn't an accident."

She hadn't noticed Detective Stiving sitting in the corner booth until he spoke up. "Looking more and more like that's the case," he said.

A moment later, Dallas strolled in, surveying the group

with quiet amusement and causing Mia to wonder about the timing.

"Well, Sam, seems like business is picking up," Dallas said.

Stiving chewed a pickle spear. "What do you want?"

Dallas arched an eyebrow. "A sandwich. Isn't that why you're here?" He smiled at Sam. "The usual, my good man."

"Vegetarian with extra mustard and no eggplant, heavy on the jalapenos," Sam rattled off.

Dallas slouched into a chair, long legs extended. "Don't let me interrupt."

Mia felt the twin pangs of affection and irritation at seeing Dallas there. She wanted the man out of her life, yet why did something inside her warm up whenever he appeared? Was he keeping tabs on her? The thought both infuriated and tantalized her.

Focus, would you? "I'll just fill this out," she said to Sam, making her way to a chair well away from Dallas.

Stiving followed her. "You might not want to take a new job, just yet."

Something about the gleam in his eye worried her. "Why?"

"Because it seems you're an heiress."

She blinked. "What are you talking about?"

"Just got word that Cora left her house and property to you. Of course, the house is pretty messed up, but the twenty acres of property, well that's worth a nice tidy sum, I'll bet."

Mia realized her mouth was hanging open. "Cora left her property to me?"

"Does that surprise you?"

"Of course it does. I had no idea."

"That right?" He wiped his thick fingers on a paper napkin. Graying chest hair puffed out at the top of his uniform shirt. "No idea at all?"

"None. What are you implying?"

"Cops, you know, look at these things called motives. Inheriting a nice chunk of land is motive."

"For what?" Mia managed to squeak out.

"For murder," he said with a smile.

Dallas moved closer when it seemed as though Mia was unable to marshal a response. "What do you have that points in that direction?"

Stiving leveled a derisive look at him. "Not that it's your business, but the coroner's initial take is that Cora didn't die from the fire."

Mia let out a little cry, her face gone deadly pale.

Dallas tensed. "Cause?"

Stiving stretched against the upholstered booth. "That's as much as I'm going to say right now. You all have a great day. I'll be in touch. Soon."

He left. Dallas realized that Sam had been standing just behind them holding a sandwich on a plastic plate. "Uh, well, I'm real sorry and all that, Mia, but maybe Stiving is right. With everything going on, it doesn't seem like a good time to have you start working here."

He shoved the plate at Dallas and waddled back to the kitchen.

Dallas dropped money on the counter, no tip, and left the sandwich on the table. By the time he'd finished, Mia had made her way outside, sinking onto a brick planter, oblivious to Juno, who had been watching through the window the whole time, swabbing an eager tongue over her hand.

Dallas sat next to her. Dark clouds overhead promised more rain and dulled the soft brown of her eyes. Or maybe it was the shock that did it. What to say to comfort her in the present situation eluded him, so he went with his gut.

"They don't have any proof. He's trying to rattle you."

The words seemed to startle her. "He thinks she was poisoned with the pills I got for her."

"Speculation and proof are two different things."

"Juno knew there was something in those pills."

"Doesn't mean you put it there."

She pressed shaking hands to her mouth. "I can't believe it. He wants to put me in jail. I can't go to jail, Dallas."

Her voice broke and it killed him. "You won't."

"But my past…isn't lily white."

"Whose is?" He wanted to smooth away the furrow between her brows, the agony in her expression. "It was self-defense before. Totally different. Your ex admits that now."

Her eyes rounded. "Have you been studying my past?"

Smooth, Dallas. Why don't you explain how you know every detail of her life? He went for casual. "Heard it somewhere."

She was too upset to think more about it. "Maybe I should leave here," she whispered. "Go back to Florida."

His pulse accelerated the tiniest bit. He said as gently as he could, "Thought you wanted a fresh start."

"Away from the Sandoval name," she finished. "I do, but my past seems to have followed me here."

And did her husband's past have anything to do with her current situation? He did not see how it could, but it was his job to find out. He'd made a promise. "There was someone else at Cora's house who could have tampered with the pills. We just have to figure out who the woman in the photo is."

Mia chewed her lip. "This is a nightmare."

"We'll fix it."

Her eyes flickered at the pronoun.

We? When had loner Dallas Black begun to think of

them as partners? The only partner he'd ever really trusted was the kind covered with fur and with a tendency to slobber. "Look who's just hit town," he said as Gracie broke away from Tina and ran to them, splashing through the puddles on the sidewalk.

"Hi, Mr. Dallas. Hi, Mommy. I'm here," she announced, heading straight for Juno to give him an ear rub. "Tina said we could get ice cream."

Mia recovered herself to give Tina a stern look.

The girl shrugged. "Sorry. I can't say no to those dimples."

"I can," Mia said, her mouth twisting in sadness. "But I won't. I think I could use a scoop, too."

"Mr. Dallas, come on," Gracie said, tugging on his hand. "We can get some for Juno."

Mia's look was enough to discourage him. "I've got to go right now, Gracie. Maybe another time."

Mia's slight nod affirmed he'd made the right choice, so why did his heart tell him otherwise? He moved close to Mia, talking low in her ear and trying not to breathe in a lungful of her shampoo-scented hair. "I've got a friend who works at the police department. I'll go see what I can find out."

She put a hand on his biceps. "I don't want to ask you to do that for me."

"You didn't ask."

He heard her sigh, sad as the sound of a blues song, as she led Gracie away without looking back, her shoulders hunched against the storm-washed sky.

Mia tried to keep Gracie occupied with the ice cream parlor and the park, but all the while her mind was racing. The police thought she'd killed her dearest friend. How could it be happening? And to inherit when Cora had blood relatives to whom she could pass her estate?

The only spot of comfort was Dallas, and she had to steel herself against any connection, no matter how much she craved it. Still, she thought she could remember the feel of his hard muscled arm under her fingers—strong, solid, the steady warmth in his eyes.

You've seen eyes like those before, remember, Mia?

Rain began to fall a little after five, and she zipped Gracie's jacket and insisted they return to the car where a nasty surprise awaited her. Her rear tire was flat all the way to the rim.

"Great. I must have driven over a screw or something." With a heavy sigh, she gave her purse to Gracie to hold and got the jack and lug wrench from the trunk. Two gentlemen and a young couple out walking their dog stopped and offered help, but Mia waved with a cheer she did not feel and finished the job herself. The effort took much longer than it should have and it was nearly sundown when she cleansed her grease-stained hands with one of her endless supply of disinfectant wipes and took the road toward home.

Gracie sang "Where Does the Ladybug Live?" as the miles went by and Mia even joined in for a while, but, as darkness fell, her stress returned. No job, no way to pay the rent and now a replacement tire needed to be purchased.

Gritting her teeth, she forced the worry down deep.

"I'm hungry," Gracie announced as they pulled into the garage.

"How can you be hungry when you ate two scoops of ice cream?"

Gracie twisted a strand of hair while she thought about it. "Dunno, but I am."

"Mac and cheese?"

The little girl nodded as she helped Mia unbuckle her car seat straps.

Mia mentally inventoried the pantry cupboard, hard to keep stocked with a voracious babysitter and child. Fortunately, there was one box left of nature's most perfect food. She helped Gracie from the car and hit the button to close the garage door.

Mia noted the interior door was unlocked, probably because Tina simply could not be induced to lock it. Mia sighed. Oh, to be an innocent eighteen-year-old again. Gracie pulled out her step stool and disappeared into the pantry.

Suddenly, the burdens of the day crashed in on Mia and she felt much older than her twenty-eight years. And why shouldn't she as the ex-wife of a drug runner and now the object of suspicion for her friend's death? *Murder, murder,* the word crawled through her mind. Tears threatened, but she would not allow them, not for a moment. Mothers did not have the luxury of folding up like tents. A shower. A quick five minute shower would wash off the grime from the day.

Hanging her purse on the kitchen hook and plugging in her cell phone to charge, she headed for the bedroom, removing her jacket. Finger poised on the light switch, she froze. A shadow was silhouetted in front of the window, just for a second before it slithered behind the cover of the drapes. Someone was in her bedroom.

Fear rushed hot into her gut, firing her nerves as she ran down the hallway. Behind her she could hear the swish of fabric as the intruder detached from the curtains. Feet thudded across the carpeted floor, her own clattering madly on the wood planked hallway as she raced for the kitchen, sweeping up her purse and grabbing Gracie who was shaking the box of macaroni and singing.

She seized her daughter with such force she heard the breath whoosh out of her, but Mia paid no heed. The man was in the hallway now, only a few feet behind her. Mia burst into the garage, hit the button and dove into the driver's side, shoving Gracie over onto the passenger seat and cranking the ignition.

The interior garage door opened, and the man appeared—thin, white, crew cut. She saw him reach for the button to stop the door from opening. She would be trapped, she and Gracie, at the mercy of this stranger.

No, she thought savagely, flipping the brights on. He flinched, throwing a hand over his eyes. The door was nearly half open now. Only a few more inches and she could get out.

Terror squeezed her insides as she saw him recover and reach for the button again.

Hurry, hurry, she commanded the groaning metal gears.

This time when he reached for the button, he succeeded and the door stopped its upward progress.

He pressed it again and it began to slide down, sealing off their escape.

FOUR

Dallas listened to the rain pounding down on the metal roof of the twenty-nine-foot trailer he rented. It was a gem of a unit as far as he was concerned, far enough away from the other trailer park residents that he enjoyed the illusion of solitude. That and the fact that the river just at the edge of the property had already persuaded many folks to temporarily relocate to another trailer park on higher ground. He wasn't completely familiar with Colorado weather patterns, but he'd give it a good couple of days before he needed to grab his pack and head for another spot.

Dallas sprawled on his back on the narrow bunk, Juno snoring on his mat on the floor. His thoughts wandered back to Mia and the fire. His police contact hadn't been able to tell him much, but he knew that circumstantial evidence could convict a person in the eyes of the law and the community.

Motive and means. Mia had both.

He got to his feet and took up his guitar from the closet. Juno burrowed deeper into his mat as Dallas strummed out a few chords on the instrument that was a gift from his brother, Trey. So, indirectly, was Dallas's damaged spleen and knee, but he did not hold that against his brother anymore. Dallas got into gang life to emulate Trey, but no one had forced him.

He'd gone in willingly and come out so damaged he would never realize his dream of being a Marine like their father.

He tried to remember his sixteen-year-old self, armed and patrolling the ten-block territory as a sentinel of sorts, a lookout for Uncle, the older leader of the gang who pedaled dope, which kept the wheels rolling. He'd admired Uncle, feared him even, yet watched him hand out new shoes and Fourth of July fireworks to the kids who couldn't afford either. They were the same kids who would be members one day, looking for that combination of belonging and protection that Uncle provided. Sixteen years old, carrying a gun, drinking and protecting a hoodlum's drug business. He cringed at the memory. What an idiot. What a coward.

How many trailers had he stayed in over the years? How many apartments or cabins had he called home until people got to know him a little too well and he felt that restless urge to move on? Was he still looking for that place to belong?

Or was it more cowardice? Probably, God forgive him. It was safer not to get to know people and to prevent them from knowing him. Safe…with a helping of sin mixed in. His grandfather's favorite baseball player, Mickey Mantle, said gangs were where cowards went to hide. Maybe they sometimes went to trailer parks, too. He fought the rising tide of self-recrimination with a muttered prayer.

The clock reminded him he hadn't eaten dinner. The fridge didn't offer much so he grabbed a rainbow of hot peppers and an onion. Armed with a perfectly balanced knife, he allowed himself to be soothed by the precision of the slices as they fell away onto the cutting board.

Juno surged to his feet, ears cocked.

Company.

So late? And in the throes of a pounding rain? He put

down the knife and sidled to the window, peering through the blinds. Nothing. No cars visible, but then his windows faced the tree-lined creek so he wouldn't see one anyway. Juno was standing in front of the door, staring with laser-like precision, ears swiveling, as if he could see beyond the metal if he just worked hard enough at it. With hearing four times greater than a human's, Juno was not often wrong about what he heard.

Dallas tried to peer through the blinds again, but the angle was wrong. Still no one knocked. Juno maintained his ferocious intensity, which told Dallas someone was out there. The slightest sound or scent telegraphed to a dog just as strongly as a stiff-knuckled rap on the door.

Okay. Let's play. Dallas gripped the door handle. Juno's whiskers quivered, body trembling, sensing a game in the offing. Juno, like every great SAR dog, had an intense play drive that never wound down.

Dallas did a slow count to three and yanked the handle.

Wind barreled in along with a gust of rain, and Juno charged down the metal stairs onto the wooden porch. He turned in circles looking for something that wasn't there.

Dallas kept his fists ready and gave the dog the moment he needed to get his bearings. Moisture-laden air confused Juno's senses, but not for long.

The dog shoved his head in the gap under the trailer and began to bark for all he was worth, tail whirling.

A woman's scream cut through the storm.

"Sit," Dallas yelled to Juno, who complied with a reluctant whine.

"Whoever you are under the trailer, come out."

No answer.

"If you don't come out, the dog is coming in."

Now there was movement, a raspy breathing, a set of slender fingers wrapping around the edge of the trailer, the impression of a face.

"He'll bite me."

Dallas called Juno to him and held the dog by the collar, more to assure the woman than out of fear that Juno would disobey. Juno didn't bite people. He was more interested in getting them to throw a ball for him to fetch. "Come out."

She emerged, soggy and mud streaked, her hair plastered in coils against her face. Red hair.

"You were there at the fire."

She didn't answer, trembling in the falling rain.

"Come inside. We'll talk."

She didn't move. "Are you a friend of Cora's?"

"Are you?" He could see the thoughts racing through her mind as she chewed her lip without answering. "All I can tell you is I won't hurt you."

"How do I know I can trust you?" she said through chattering teeth.

"Guess you can't. You came here to find me and here I am. If you want to talk, we do it inside. Don't want the dog to catch cold."

After another long look at Juno, the woman ran up the steps.

He tossed her a towel, which she wrapped around her shoulders before she sank onto the kitchen chair. Juno did his thing, sniffing her muddy shoes and the hem of her sodden linen pants.

Dallas studied her while he heated water in the microwave and flung in a tea bag which had come with the trailer. Some sort of fruity herbal stuff. Her clothes had been nice at one point, ruined now. A light jacket was not up to the task of keeping her dry from the pummeling rain. No purse.

"Who are you?" he asked as he handed her the tea.

She clutched it between her shaking hands, her knuckles white.

"Susan." She swallowed. "I was going to meet Cora, and I saw the house burning. I tried to get inside to help her."

Nice story. "Why were you meeting her?"

"She was...looking into something for me." She locked eyes on his, hers a pale gray. "Is she all right?"

Dallas considered. Time to find out if Susan really was a friend to Cora. "Dead." He gauged her reaction.

The woman did not move, as if the words were lost in the steam from the mug she held to her lips. "Dead."

"So why were you going to see her?"

She gazed into the tea. "How did the fire start?"

"Maybe I should be asking you that."

She jerked. "You think I set it?"

"So far I've seen you running away from a fire and sneaking outside my trailer. Puts your character in question."

A glimmer of a smile lifted her lips, but there was something under the trailing wet hair, behind the gaunt lines of her mouth that revealed a hardness he hadn't seen at first. "So you're wondering if you can trust me?" she said.

"Not wondering. I'm not going to trust you, not until you give me the truth."

"You're a hard man."

He sat opposite her. "I've got peppers to sauté. What are you here for?"

She held his eyes with hers, a slight lift to her chin. "Justice."

"Not easy to find."

"I know. But I'm going to have it. I'm going to get back what belongs to me." The last words came out as a hiss.

"What were you doing at Cora's?"

"Meeting her there. She was trying to help me unmask a villain, so to speak."

"Who?"

"It's private."

He rapped a hand on the table. "We're wasting time. Cora was likely murdered and you were there at the scene."

"If I was going to kill someone, or burn a house in this town," she said, after drinking deeply of the tea, "that's not the one I would have picked. And by the way, you were there, too, at the scene. Did you have something to do with Cora's death?"

Dallas resisted the urge to raise his voice. "If you thought I did, a quick phone call to the police would take care of it. You came here for another reason."

"I wanted to know about Cora, and I'm not asking the police for personal reasons."

Very personal, judging from the flicker of emotion that pinched the corners of her mouth. Impasse. They'd gotten there, he could tell. Whatever her motives, he wasn't going to pry them out of her. Women didn't work that way, he'd learned. Instead he sat back in the chair and waited.

Mia's mouth went dry as the garage door stopped with a groan, halfway up. The man hopped off the step and ran to the car. He was coming to drag her out. The old car had no automatic locks so she slammed the button down and realized in a hot wave of panic that he was not headed to her side, but Gracie's.

"Lock the door, Gracie," Mia shouted.

Gracie sat frozen, staring at her mother.

Mia dove across her and hammered the lock, the back door, as well. The man banged his palms against the glass.

Gracie screamed. "Stop, stop!"

Mia nearly screamed too until the man stepped away suddenly. He picked up a metal bucket and swung it hard at the passenger window with a deafening crash until the glass was etched through with cracks.

"Get down onto the floor," Mia yelled to Gracie, "and cover your head with your hands."

She yanked the car into Reverse. After one quick breath, she stomped on the gas. The car shot backwards into the garage door. There was a terrible moment when the roof met the unyielding mass and she thought she had made a fatal error. Groaning metal, the sound of breaking glass and then quite without warning the car punched through, shearing the garage door into a crumpled mess, exploding onto the rain-slicked driveway.

Mia was oblivious to the damage. Only two facts remained, her car was still functioning and they were free from the garage. She reversed down the slope, cranked the car into Drive and sped off down the road, putting as much distance between the man and Gracie as she possibly could. One mile, two, her stomach remained in a tight knot, fingers clenched around the steering wheel.

She forced several breaths in and out before she could coax her voice into action. "Gracie Louise, are you hurt?"

Gracie's tiny voice floated up from the floor. "Scary."

"You're right," she said, relief making her voice thick. "But it's okay now. You can climb back on the seat. Be careful of the glass."

Gracie emerged like a hare having narrowly escaped the fox. Her lips were parted, eyes wide and wet. "Mommy, that was a bad man."

Mia gave a shaky laugh and took her daughter's hand. "Yes, he was."

"Why was he in our house?"

She swallowed. "I don't know, but we'll go someplace safe until we find out, okay?"

"Where?"

The million dollar question. The nearest hotel was an hour away, and they didn't have the money to stay in one for long anyway. Rain splattered through the side window that had broken when it impacted the garage door. She felt the bitter tide of anger rise as she contemplated her own helplessness. Mia risked a quick stop, engine running, to move Gracie to the backseat and buckle her into her booster. She kissed her and caressed her daughter's plump cheeks. "I'm going to figure out something, okay?"

Gracie nodded, shaking the box of macaroni she still clung to. "But I'm hungry."

Mia smiled as she climbed back into the driver's seat, but worry soon overwhelmed her. She didn't even have a cell phone to call the police. The storm intensified as she drove along, rattling the sides of the car. If she could call her sister for advice...

Your sister who is busy with her new husband and her new life. They were tight now, together again after all the anguish Mia had caused, but still there remained in the shadows between them, a heavy weight of guilt. It stemmed from the fact that her sister had been right about Hector when Mia refused to hear a bad word about him, a feeling that burgeoned during her time in jail with all its horrors. Because of Hector, Antonia was almost killed and there was nobody to blame for bringing him into their lives but Mia. No, she would not call Antonia.

"Why not call Hector?" her derisive thoughts chided her. He was sitting around in prison with nothing much to do and a reach that seemed to exceed the metal walls that caged him. She could grovel even more and throw herself on Dr. Elias's mercy. Was there any pride left to salvage? Self-pity gave way to a hot flood of determination.

Stand on your own two feet, for once in your life.

Mile after mile gave her no clarity, no better sense of what to do. Only the instinct to keep going, to get away from whoever had violated their home, kept her pressing the car forward. She'd made up her mind to stop at the next town she came to and call the police when she realized where she was, at the entrance to the trailer park where

Dallas lived. She'd given him a lift there once when his truck had engine trouble.

She saw the silhouette of his vehicle, and she pulled her car next to it, motor still running.

"Where are we?" Gracie said, unbuckling her strap.

"Nowhere, I was just stopping to rest my eyes for a minute." What was she doing? She would not go to Dallas for help, the man who already seemed to have a strange influence over her pulse. An image of long-stemmed yellow roses floated into her mind. It was followed by a vision of Hector, the man whom she'd loved desperately, blindly, the husband who lied to her from the first kiss and right on until his arrest for drug dealing and later for the attempted abduction of her sister. *Fool, fool, fool.* Tears brimmed, captive in her eyes.

She swallowed hard. "Put your seat belt back on, we're not stopping here."

"But there's Juno," Gracie gabbled, shoving open the door and hopping out.

"Get back in the car right now, Gracie Louise," Mia said, noting the spill of light from Dallas's door as he emerged onto the trailer steps, peering into the darkness.

"Hi, Dallas," Gracie called. "Can you make me some mac and cheese?"

Mia sighed. God could not lead her to another dark-haired man who would prove her a fool again. If that was His plan, Mia was going to make one of her own. Jaw tense, she stepped out of the car and went to retrieve her daughter.

FIVE

"Sorry to bother you," Mia said, forcing a light tone, as Dallas bent to talk to Gracie, Juno dancing on eager paws beside him.

"Someone broke into our house," Gracie said. "I think it was the Boogeyman. He wanted this." She thrust the box of mac and cheese up in the rain.

Dallas's face was a picture of confusion. "Huh?" he finally managed.

Mia squished up to him, feet sinking into the grass. "We had a break-in. We're going to the next town to call the cops."

It was hard to read his expression through the sheeting rain. "Come inside."

Gracie hooted her approval and headed for the trailer.

"No," Mia said too quickly. "I mean, we don't want to involve you. I can handle it." She wished her teeth had not begun to chatter madly at that moment.

"You can handle it inside, out of the rain."

"I appreciate the offer."

"Inside then." And that was that. Dallas turned his back and ushered Gracie and Juno up the steps, politely holding the door for Mia, his muscled forearm gleaming wetly. And what was a woman on the edge of desperation supposed to do about that?

Just a phone call. A quick stop to rest and then out. She squelched up the trailer steps and inside, stopping abruptly in the doorway until he came up behind and pushed her gently through.

"I'll leave puddles."

His gaze flickered around the tidy interior. "You won't be the first one." He sighed. "Gone."

"Who?"

"The redhead from the fire. Name's Susan. She came here."

Mia gasped. "What did she want? Who is she?"

He shrugged. "Not the chatty type. Only got that she was meeting Cora and she has some big trust issues. She was sitting at the table when I heard you pull up. She must have snuck out." He leveled a look at Juno. "Aren't you supposed to alert me to people sneaking around, dog?"

Juno shook water from his thick coat and hurled himself on the floor to offer his belly to Gracie for scratching.

Mia giggled.

Dallas did not, but she thought there was a slight quirk on his lips. Mia made one more trip into the rain to fetch the bag of spare clothes she kept in the car. In a few moments, Gracie was wearing faded jeans and a T-shirt, one size too small but dry.

"Can you make this?" Gracie said, shaking the box of macaroni at Dallas.

"What is it?"

The child blinked. "It's mac and cheese. Don'tcha eat that?"

"No," Dallas said.

"Well, what do you eat?" she demanded.

"Spicy food that makes you sweat. But I can probably manage mac and cheese."

"No need," Mia said.

Flood Zone

Dallas pointed to the tiny bathroom. "There's a sweatshirt hanging on a hook in there. It's ugly, but dry."

"We're not staying."

"I got that. Go put on something dry anyway. I don't think I can enjoy eating this mac stuff while you're dripping all over the floor." He turned to Gracie. "How do you cook it? The label's blurry from the rain."

"Dump the stuff in bubbling water," Gracie sang out as Mia headed to the bathroom.

"Don't get too close to Juno," she warned Gracie. "He'll get mad if you pester him."

Dallas quirked an eyebrow. "He's never mad at kids, but I'll watch them anyway."

Mia walked into the bathroom and leaned her head against the door. *Safe. You're safe for the moment, and so is Gracie.* She wanted to whisper a prayer, but something hardened the words in her throat. *You got yourself out of that jam, Mia, and you can handle whatever comes next. All by yourself.*

She squeezed the water out of her hair and slicked it down straight as best she could. Rolling up her sodden shirt, she pulled on the soft gray sweatshirt that went down past her knees. It felt warm against her skin.

She emerged to find Dallas in deep discussion with Gracie as she stared at the pile of jigsaw puzzle pieces set out on a piece of plywood that served as a table.

"I don't know what it's going to be," Dallas said.

Gracie blinked. "But what's the picture on the box?"

"A mouse chewed the box, so I put the pieces in a plastic bag. Can't remember what the picture is."

She touched a piece with one soft fingertip. "You haven't gotten many pieces together."

He nodded, staring ruefully at the corner where a half dozen pieces were connected. "I move a lot. Gotta put it away each time."

"How long have you been working on it?" Mia asked.

He squinted. "Going on twelve years now."

She wasn't sure whether to gasp or laugh. "Really?"

"Well, I think it's going to be a dog puzzle," Gracie said.

"Could be. My mother gave it to me for my fifteenth birthday. She can't remember what the picture was, either." He sniffed. "Is mac and cheese supposed to smell like that?"

They looked at the pot which was bubbling madly on the stove. Mia grabbed a potholder and took it off the heat. There were bits of packaging swirling through the noodles and grainy orange tinted water. "Uh-oh. You dumped in the cheese envelope."

"The what?"

"I forgot to tell him," Gracie wailed. "You're not 'posed to put the cheese envelope in the water."

Mia put the mess into the sink. "I'm afraid it's ruined."

Dallas sighed. "I should have paid better attention while I was dumping. Who puts cheese in an envelope anyway?"

Gracie sat forlornly next to Juno. "Awww, rats."

"Hang on," Dallas said, wrenching open the cupboard. "I just remembered something." He held a bag of Goldfish triumphantly in the air. "How about some of these?"

Gracie cheered, and Mia had to laugh as he handed Gracie the crackers with all the solemnity of a professor awarding a diploma. "Just don't feed too many to the dog," he said.

After a moment of hesitation, he said to Mia, "I'm making tofu and peppers. Share them with me?" She had not shared a private meal with a man since her disastrous marriage. Sweat popped out on her forehead.

"Oh, I couldn't."

"There's no meat, but I've got plenty." His black eyes fastened on her.

Mia was a committed carnivore, but how could she

say no to the man whose sweatshirt she was wearing and who had massacred a box of mac and cheese in an effort to feed her child?

"Yes," she said humbly. "That would be very nice."

"Here's a phone to call the cops. Then you can tell me about what happened."

She sank down at the table. "You're not going to believe me."

"Try…" His words trailed off as he scanned the kitchen counter.

"What's wrong?"

"Before she took off, Susan helped herself."

"To your dinner?"

"No," he said, voice low and deep. "To my knife."

Dallas kept the words low so Gracie wouldn't hear, but he needn't have worried. She was deep in conversation with Juno about the merits of some or other Goldfish flavor over the rest.

He selected another knife from the block and began slicing peppers, while Mia phoned the police. There was no way to avoid listening in and that was fine since he was itching to know the details of what sent Mia and Gracie out into the night. To him.

Was she really there in his trailer, rolling her damp hair into a ponytail? He nearly nicked his finger trying to take a sideways glance at her.

Mia explained the break-in to the dispatcher and gave Dallas's cell number as a contact before hanging up.

"They'll send a unit when they can, but the levee is failing just north of town." She laughed, a bitter sound. "They may need to evacuate my neighborhood anyway. It's true what they say, when it rains, it pours."

He dumped the peppers into sizzling olive oil and applied himself to neatly cubing the silken tofu. "It's not a coincidence. Guy was looking for something, maybe."

"Or looking to…" Her voice trailed away.

He stirred the pan with a wooden spoon. "I think he was searching and you surprised him. You said you had a flat. My guess is he made that happen to buy some time so he could search."

"For what? Why?" Her lips parted in exasperation, dark eyes flashing. He found his own mouth had gone dry.

"Could it be connected to the fire?" Mia pressed her hands to her forehead. "I don't even know what Cora was looking into. She didn't give me the slightest clue."

"Yes, she did," he said, sliding a plate in front of her.

Mia gasped. "The photo. It's in a file drawer. I have to go back and get it."

"In the morning. Sleep here. Juno and I will find an empty unit, and you can have this one."

"No, we couldn't displace you."

He sat on a chair across from her. "You're tired, and Gracie needs a safe place to sleep."

He could see the struggle unfold across her face in magnificent waves. "Mia, I'm not pressuring you to do anything. I'm just offering a safe place to sleep until morning. That's all."

She bit her lip.

He took her hand, the delicate fingers cool in his own. "Let's pray." He closed his eyes and thanked the Lord for keeping Gracie and Mia safe and for the provision of food and shelter. When he straightened, he thought he could see a million thoughts, a cascading river of emotions rolling through her eyes.

"I wouldn't guess you to be the kind to pray."

"Yeah? Because I'm a troublemaker?"

"No, no, of course not." She laughed. "Well, maybe a little."

"Troublemakers need God more than most." He picked up his fork and started to eat.

She did the same. "Wow, hot." She panted, reaching for a glass of water.

"Sorry." He handed her a piece of bread. "Water doesn't really help much. I've done a lot of backpacking. Spicy adds flavor to camping food." He considered the contents of the fridge. "I have some eggs. I'll scramble you some."

He started to rise, but she stopped him with a touch on his arm that seemed to ignite an odd flicker of nerves all the way up to his shoulder.

"This is fine." She swallowed. "Hector…loved spicy food, too, I just haven't had it in a while. Thank you for cooking it for me."

He should have gone with the eggs. "Do you worry about what he'll do when he's out?"

She swallowed and wiped her mouth with a paper napkin. "He already knows too much about my life, even from prison."

And Hector's enemies did, too. He had squirreled away money, so the rumor went, a hefty sum extorted or swindled from his competitors, including the ferocious Garza family. Garza wanted it back and he'd sent out feelers to discover if Mia knew the whereabouts of the jackpot. Could be the guy who broke into her house wasn't searching for the photo, but the money.

A friendly DEA agent had alerted Reuben and Antonia to Garza's interest. And Antonia had hired Dallas to keep tabs on Mia. Dallas was good at watching people, finding the lost—fighting—if necessary, and skirting rules when they did not serve. He had no home, no ties. He was the perfect man for the job.

And Mia would despise him when she found out. He speared another slice of pepper.

For now, he would allow himself to savor the relative

closeness between them, a feeling he had not experienced in a very long time. It was a shame that staring was bad manners, because all he really wanted to do was sit motionless and drink her in.

Her gaze was soft as she watched Gracie play with Juno, feeding him way more Goldfish than any dog should consume. When a gust of rain hammered on the metal roof with such force that it boomed through the trailer, Gracie ran to her mother's arms.

"It's okay, baby," Mia crooned. "Just the rain."

"Where's the bad man?"

Mia exchanged a quick look with Dallas.

"Bad man isn't going to come here," Dallas said.

"Why?"

"Because Juno is big and scary, and so am I."

Gracie smiled and hopped in his lap. He was so startled he didn't know what to do, sitting there as if he had a live grenade on his knees. Should he stand up? Give her a pat? Instead he sat rigid, hands raised, like a complete dork.

She grabbed him around the neck and pasted a cheesy kiss on his cheek. "I'm glad we came here."

So am I, his heart supplied, much to the surprise of his mind, but he was still relieved when she vacated his lap.

He saw to the details as best he could, thinking his mother would have played the job of host much better than he. Extra blankets for Mia and Gracie, heater turned on to a low hum to ward off the chill. Couple of clean towels in case anybody needed showering. Was there something else? Antacids, to cure any hot pepper damage. And magazines? *Wilderness Survival*. Did women like that sort of thing? He stood awkwardly in the doorway.

"Keep my phone here." He pulled out a spare he always had handy and programmed his cell into the one he gave Mia. "Call if you need anything. Use the laptop if you want. You can sign on as a guest."

Gracie crimped her lips. "What if the bad man comes while you're gone?" she whispered.

He considered telling her about the trailer he would sleep in across the way which gave him a direct line of sight that he intended to monitor on a regular basis. There were other things he could share, but he did not. "You want Juno to stay with you?"

"Yes." Gracie nodded, hopping from foot to foot. "Juno will watch me sleep."

"Actually, he'll sleep, too."

Mia shot him a look that indicated he probably should have kept that fact to himself. How was someone supposed to know what to divulge to a kid and what not to? Was there some kind of instruction manual?

"Juno will sleep, but he hears things that you can't."

"Like bad men?"

Dallas nodded.

"If he hears me, how will he know I'm not bad?"

"He just knows."

"Like God?"

Dallas took in the little bow of a mouth, the sweet innocence in that sober gaze and something moved inside him. "Yes, Gracie. God made dogs smart that way."

"My daddy's bad," Gracie whispered, so low he almost didn't hear it.

He heard Mia gasp, her lips pressed together. He swallowed and sent up a little prayer that he wouldn't say something stupid and took a knee. "Your daddy made mistakes. If he's sorry, God will help him be a good man again."

"God can do that?" she said, eyebrow raised.

"Yes, He can."

"How do you know?"

Dallas blew out a breath. "Because I was a bad man, and God helped me to be good again." Gracie gave him a long, serious look, then hugged him.

Mia wrapped her arms around herself. Had he made things better? Or worse? He could not tell from the expression on her face. Without another word that might tip the balance to one side or the other, he let himself out into the rain.

SIX

The night droned on. Rain hammered down and thoughts thundered through Mia's mind, three words pinching uncomfortably at her heart.

My daddy's bad.

Hector had done terrible things. He was bad, in some ways, but he had nearly died trying to save her sister from the trap he'd set for her on the island. He'd gone to prison, professing he would come out a better man. They had no future together, nothing that should stir her toward forgiveness. She would never love him again. The rage and hatred inside her would stay forever, she feared, blackening and staining her whole life. If Hector was bad, unforgivable, unredeemable, what did that mean for the child he had fathered? Or the wife who'd made so many mistakes herself?

And what of Dallas? She knew only a small bit about his troubled youth, but without question she was also certain Dallas Black was a good man. Then again, she'd thought Hector was, too.

Mia felt the soft rise and fall of Gracie's breathing, her back curled against Mia's stomach on the narrow bunk bed. How small she was, this little girl who looked to Mia to show her who God was, a god of forgiveness. It was something Mia could say with her mouth, but not embrace in her soul.

If he's sorry, God will help him be a good man again.

She wondered afresh about the strange and straightforward Dallas Black. The troublemaker with a certainty about himself and God that she could no longer deny attracted her. She itched to soothe her restlessness with movement. Careful not to wake Gracie, Mia crept from the bed, earning an intense look from Juno who was stationed on the floor.

He stared at her, pupils two glimmers in the dimness. Dogs were strange to her, galumphing creatures who made messes and were prone to biting. The big lumbering animal scared her a bit, but he undeniably enchanted Gracie for some reason. Slobbery tongue, muddy paws, sharp teeth.

And a friend, to a child who had no others.

She crouched down next to the animal. "Thank you, Juno," she whispered.

The dog swiveled his ears, considering, and then laid his head back on his paws and assumed his watchful rest.

She clicked on the small light above the kitchen table and powered up Dallas's laptop, navigating to her inbox. While the computer booted up, she peered out the blinds into the unceasing rain. Across the way, a dim yellow light gleamed from the window of Dallas's trailer. It made her feel better to know he was there and at the same time grateful there was a safe distance between them.

The previous day played back in her mind like a bad movie. Cora gone and so was her job. Dr. Elias's face flashed in her memory. Had she misread the whole situation? Had he really been offering help? Trust your instincts, Dallas told her. But she trusted nothing about herself anymore, especially where men were concerned.

Pulling her attention back to the laptop, she opened her inbox. A message from her sister.

How are you? Hurricane cleanup continues here. Reuben is confident that he can start replanting the orchard soon.

The man lives, eats and breathes oranges. How did I get fixed up with a guy who loves oranges more than me?

Mia smiled. Reuben loved his orchard, but they both knew that the man was desperately in love with Antonia. She felt the pang of envy. Hector had loved her, too, in his own way, but he'd loved power and money more.

I hear there is flooding in your area. Come to visit us in Florida. Aside from the odd hurricane, we've got perfect weather. We'll put you to work, but you'll be above water. I'd feel better if I could keep my eyes on you.

Antonia knew that Hector tracked Mia everywhere. And Hector's enemies? The people he'd cheated and double-crossed? Did they track her everywhere, too? A shiver rippled up her spine and she read the remainder of the message.

I know you don't want me to do the protective big sister thing. I'll try to be good, I promise. Reuben wants you here, too. He misses Gracie, and he wants to see her climb a tree. Waiting for your reply. A

Mia's fingers stiffened over the keyboard. See Gracie climb a tree? How did her sister know Gracie had managed to clamber up the old cottonwood tree in the backyard of their rented house a few days prior? The child was bursting with pride, even though Dallas had to get a ladder to fetch her down, and reported the accomplishment to everyone who crossed their path in the small town. Was Antonia having someone spy on her? Teeth gritted, she forced out several measured breaths.

She was turning into a nutcase. Reuben's life was trees. Of course he'd want to see Gracie climb one. She read the email again. The tree-climbing reference was purely co-incidental, and her paranoia was turning her against the one person she knew was completely on her side. Hitting Reply, she contemplated how to put into words all that had happened the past two days.

Cora is dead. I am under suspicion for the murder. An intruder broke into our house. I'm staying in Dallas's trailer. I'm scared, worried, alone.

She perused the words that would send her sister into a panic. The sister who had been right all along. The woman who deserved above everyone else to enjoy the start of a marriage to the man she'd loved and lost and found again.

Backspace. Delete.

Blinking back tears she typed instead:

Gracie's growing like mad. She checks her teeth every day to see if they are loose, so desperate to use the special tooth box you sent. So busy here with work and school. Will write soon. Love you and Reuben. M

The inbox was cluttered with ads and offers from every company she'd ordered from recently using a credit card with her maiden name. It was a very tiny victory, but she took comfort in the fact that she had been able to provide the bare bones necessities with her very own hard-earned cash. Thanks to a secondhand store in town, she'd even managed a plastic wading pool that had gotten them through the hot months. It was light-years from the expensive toys and top-of-the-line clothes Gracie had when she was a baby in Hector's home, but it was bought with honest money. Gracie didn't seem to realize they were living perilously close to the poverty line. Not yet, anyway.

Clearing out the junk brought her to the last email.

Her heart hammered. It could not be. The sender's name, *c.graham,* did not change no matter how hard she blinked. Cora Graham had sent her an email at four-thirty on the day she'd died, shortly after she'd sent the text summoning them to her house.

Panic squeezed Mia's stomach, and for a moment, she was too terrified to click open the email. Finally, with fingers gone cold, she did.

Find P. Finnigan. He knows the truth. I can't...

The message ended abruptly. Mia's heart pounded. Cora had sent the message when? As the smoke overcame her? As the poison paralyzed her body and she realized she could not escape?

Sobs wrenched through Mia. She clapped a hand over her mouth to keep from waking Gracie and staggered to the porch, stepping outside, grateful that the rain had momentarily slowed to a trickle. Sucking in deep breaths, she tried to rein in her stampeding emotions. It should not have surprised her to hear Dallas's door open. In a moment, he was next to her, peering into her face.

"Tell me," he said softly.

She couldn't answer over the grief that welled up inside.

With arms both strong and gentle, he pulled her close, not offering any more words, but the warmth and solace of his body pressed to hers.

With her head tucked under his chin, he let the mist dance lightly against his face, finding himself oddly relaxed with her in his arms. It was as if she molded naturally into his embrace, a perfect fit with a man who never fit in anywhere. He pressed his cheek against her hair and wondered if there was something he should be saying.

He went with silence. She would tell him what made her cry, or not. He would do everything in his power to help. That was all there was to it. So instead he relished the feel of her there, until the mist turned to drizzle and he guided her back into the trailer.

She wiped her face and sat at the kitchen table. He slid in across from her.

"I'm sorry," she said. "I slipped into hysteria there for a minute."

"No sweat."

"It was because of this." She turned the laptop to face him. "It's from Cora."

He read it. "Do you know a P. Finnigan?"

She shook her head, eyes huge in the near darkness. "Should we tell the police?"

"Yes. When you meet with them tomorrow. I'll work on it."

"How?"

"Let me worry about it. Get some sleep."

She offered an exasperated look. "Easy for you to say. You don't seem to need any sleep. Were you keeping watch on us all this time?"

I haven't been able to take my eyes off you since the day I met you, his fickle heart supplied. Fortunately, his mouth was still in charge. "Don't need much sleep."

"Or much furniture?"

He shrugged.

"Or a TV?"

"Too noisy." He won a smile with that one.

She rested her chin on her hand. "What do you need?"

The question surprised him. "Simple stuff. Backpack. Hot shower. Dog kibble."

That got a giggle that faded rapidly. "I mean, you move around all the time, like you're looking for something. What is it?"

How did he get himself into this sticky conversation? The silence stretched into awkward so he broke down and told her. "Ever hear that verse from Proverbs? Starts with 'trust in the Lord' and ends with 'Seek his will in all you do, and he will show you which path to take?'"

She nodded solemnly.

"Well, I tried to take my own path plenty of times, and it got me in jail and beaten badly and deep into gang life." He watched carefully to see if she would recoil. Most women did when he got around to his sorry life history. Those brown eyes stayed riveted to his face.

"Why a gang?"

"My dad died when I was a teen, and I went nuts. Joined a gang, figured it made me a man, cool, like my brother."

"But he got out, didn't he?"

"Yeah. He's smarter than me. Military straightened him out. He tried to get me out, too, but I'm hardheaded. Took the beating to do that. I woke up handcuffed to the bed, and the first thing I thought of was, had I killed someone?"

She stayed quiet.

"I hadn't. God spared me from that, but I could have." His voice hitched a little. "Oh, how easily I could have done it."

"You wanted to go into the military, didn't you? Your brother told me, I think." Her voice was soft and soothing, like water over river stones.

He sighed. "My whole life I wanted to be a Marine like my father. My choices ruined that for me. They don't take people with damaged legs and gang histories." It still hurt to say it, but somehow, telling it to her, it was more of a dull ache than a ripping pain.

"I'm sorry."

"I'm not. Oh, I wish I could have done it some other way, but destroying my life brought me to the edge of ruin and that's where I finally found God. From then on, I figured I'd let Him show me where to go and I guess He brought me here for a while."

"Until it's time to go again?"

"Dunno. He'll thump me on the head when He wants me to put down some roots." He paused. "What about you? What do you need?"

She laughed, but there was no joy in the sound. "I need a place to call home, where I can put down roots so deep Gracie and I will never be uprooted again, but I'm never going to get that."

"No?"

"No, because Hector will never leave us alone, and everywhere we go his bad choices follow us." She closed her eyes for a moment and breathed out a sigh. "No, our bad choices. I've…" She swallowed. "I've been to jail, too, and now it looks as if I might be going there again." Her face paled. "What have we done to Gracie? Two people who were supposed to love and protect her? What have we done?"

Tears sparkled there in her eyes, but she would not let them fall. *Good girl, Mia.*

He took her hands and squeezed hard. "Gracie is happy and loved. Even I can tell that, and kids are like space aliens to me."

Small smile.

"Not one person on this Earth has no regrets."

Juno thrashed in his sleep.

"Except dogs."

"That's probably true." He fell into the warmth of those eyes. "I'll help you find a place to put down roots." Dumb. The moment he said it she pulled away. Way to go, Dallas Foot-in-Mouth Black.

Her tone became careful, formal. "Thank you, but I'm going to take care of us. That's a lesson I learned the hard way. I can only count on myself."

Wrong lesson. No bigger disappointment than oneself. "Sure. I didn't mean anything by it." He looked outside.

"Sun's almost up. I'll follow you into town so you can talk to the cops."

He headed for the door, not at a run but close to it. "There are some eggs, like I said, and maybe cheese somewhere. Will Gracie eat that?"

She nodded, face still tight. "Yes, thank you. I'll replace it all when I can."

He let her have that, if it was what she needed to feel in control.

"Good night, Mia."

Two hours later he followed her bashed up car toward town. Ominous signs of disaster preparation were visible as they drove along the main street. Shop owners were filling burlap bags with sand to be piled along the embankment that would optimistically stem the flood. Mia decided to stop and retrieve the photo before meeting with the police chief, so they drove along rain-drenched streets toward the lower lying valley where she rented a home. His gut tightened as a dark-colored SUV trailed behind them along the main drag and onto the narrow two-lane road. Not cause for alarm, per se, but he thought it just might be the same SUV he'd noticed parked on the side of the road several miles back. Colorado plates. Might be a rental.

Dallas slowed and so did the SUV. Not good. Keeping a distance. Nothing to be done to lose the guy at this point. Besides, in one of his stay-up-all-night reading frenzies, hadn't he read some sage advice from a Chinese general in 400 BC about keeping your friends close and your enemies closer?

"All right," he whispered, earning an interested look from Juno in the passenger seat. He maintained a steady pace, and the car dropped back just enough to preserve the gap between them.

He braked hard when Mia stopped abruptly. In a moment, he understood. The road dipped down, following the slope of the valley, only now the asphalt had disappeared under several feet of water. The surface was muddy and rippled, speckled with leaves and broken branches. She got out, hands on hips turning to give him an exasperated look that almost made him smile.

He joined her, noting that the SUV had pulled over a half mile behind them.

"Can your truck make it across?"

"Might, but I'm not going to risk anyone's safety. There's a bridge back a ways. We'll double back."

She groaned. "That will take us another half hour."

"Better late than drowned."

She looked as though she didn't appreciate his pearls of wisdom, but she acquiesced.

Juno sniffed disinterestedly at the water, stopping a moment to eye the car behind them on the road.

A look of fear flashed across her face. "Who is that?"

"Dunno, but I'll find out in a minute. Let's head for the bridge."

Mia gave the SUV a second look. He knew she wanted to ask more questions, but instead she got behind the wheel and turned around. Dallas fell in behind her and by the time they were rolling, the SUV had disappeared. Not for long. As he predicted, it picked them up again some five miles in, once again hanging back just enough.

The bridge was of sturdy steel construction, spanning the river that was normally well below its concrete piers. Now the water lapped considerably above that mark, but not enough to leave the structure impassable.

Yet.

Dallas decided it was time to get a better handle on the situation.

Mia drove over the bridge, and when she was safely

across, he followed suit. A couple of feet in, he stomped on the brakes, bringing his vehicle to a dead stop.

"Time to come clean," he muttered, looking into the rearview as the SUV made the approach to the bridge. He stopped abruptly, too.

If their shadow was there for purely innocent reasons, he'd wait patiently, figuring there was some obstruction, maybe even honk after a bit, or try to pass. Certainly he'd get out of the car to investigate why Dallas was stopped, blocking the road.

Instead, the driver backed rapidly off the bridge, did a jerky three-point turn and took off in the other direction.

Dallas almost smiled for the second time that morning. He rolled down the window and called to Mia who had stopped and stuck her head out the window to question him.

"Go on. I'll be there soon."

Her eyes widened, quarter-size. "What are you doing?"

"Just making friends," he called out the window.

SEVEN

Dallas let the SUV outdistance him until it sped around a sharp bend in the shrub-lined road. He slowed and turned up a rough stretch which was probably more a trail than a road, but a way Dallas and Juno had explored many times in their backpacking travels. He stopped for only a moment to call a friend and give him the plate number.

"You know I got things to do 'sides hack info for you, right?" Farley said.

Dallas laughed. "Gonna help me or not?"

Farley snorted. "If you and Fido hadn't saved my life, I'd be in the bottom of a ravine with vultures using my bones for toothpicks."

"Vultures don't have teeth. Staying sober?"

"Yeah, man. Prayed myself through the last real bad stretch."

Dallas had prayed right along with him. And picked Farley up when he hadn't made it through, cleaned him up, filled him with coffee and nearly hog-tied the kid to get him to a meeting. "Gotta win, every day."

"I know, Mother, I know. Stop nagging and let me get to work."

"While you're at it, can you see if there's a P. Finnigan living in the area?"

"All right. See ya." Farley clicked off.

Dallas pushed the truck along, rocks pinging into the bottom, irritating Juno who barked just once.

"Half a mile more." Dallas squeezed the truck by a narrow section of path, branches scraping the sides, until he'd looped back out to the main road. A recent rock slide took out a bend of the highway, leaving the section blocked with a mess of boulders and only one lane passable. It was marked with cones and caution signs. Handy. He rolled down the window and listened to learn if he'd guessed correctly.

The sound of the SUV's approach told him he had. He edged past the rockfall and pulled the truck across the road. SUV guy would pass the blockage, encounter the truck and have to stop and back, which would slow him down enough for Dallas to get a good look. Risky, but with Mia's situation worsening by the minute, he needed some intel. Keep your enemies close…

The SUV was taking an unhurried pace. Dallas got out of the truck and he and Juno took a position behind a pile of rocks. Juno gave him the "you're probably crazy but I'm happy to participate in your insanity" look. They waited less than five minutes.

The SUV made the turn, stopped so fast the tires skidded a few inches. Dallas crouched low, peering over a granite lip of rock to identify the driver. To his surprise, the man shoved open the door and got out. Dallas took a picture with his cell phone.

Not much to him, but strength had nothing to do with size. Fair skin, buzz-cut hair. Tight skinny jeans and a shiny jacket that was probably fashionable somewhere in the world where Dallas hoped he never found himself.

The guy looked slowly around, hands loose at his sides. "We gonna talk?" he called out, voice higher pitched than Dallas guessed.

Dallas climbed out from behind the rock, and Juno

scampered over to the man. He gave him a careful circling before he settled on sniffing his sneakers. "You're following Mia. Why? Who are you?"

The kid had to be no more than twenty. "Archie. How do you know I'm not following you?"

Dallas considered. "I'm not worth following. Did you break into her house?"

Archie crouched slowly and offered an outstretched hand to Juno. "I love dogs. Miss mine. He's some sort of lab and husky mix. Chews my shoes when I don't walk him enough and leaves them on the bed for me to find."

Dallas waited, watching to make sure Archie didn't reach for any kind of weapon in his ridiculous excuse for a jacket. "I asked you a question."

"My boss sent me here. I do what I'm told."

"Who's your boss?"

Archie straightened. "Guy who wants his property back."

Dallas's pulse sped up a fraction. "Do you work for Hector?"

Archie laughed. "Good one. I like to be on the winning team." He checked his watch. "You're a roadblock, in more ways than one. You need to step aside."

"Not if you're after Mia."

"She has something that belongs to my boss. He wants it back. No need for any pain. Just a simple negotiation."

"She doesn't have anything, and if you hurt her, it will be the last thing you ever do." He had not raised his voice, but the intensity made Juno return to his side and sit, rigid with expectation.

"All right," Archie said, pulling out a switchblade and flicking it open. "This is as good a place to kill you as any, but I don't want to hurt the dog. Tell him not to attack."

Juno wasn't an attack dog. In fact, he was the perfect Search and Rescue dog because he was passionately interested in people, but they also had a bond that surpassed owner and worker.

"All right," Dallas said calmly. "I'll send him to fetch and then you and I can get down to business. May I?" He gestured to a stick on the ground a few feet away and Archie nodded.

Dallas bent over to get the stick and while he was at it, grabbed a palm full of gravel loosed from the earlier slide.

"Okay, Juno. Ready to fetch?"

Juno shot to his feet as Dallas tossed the stick into the trees and then turned to fire the handful of gravel at Archie who instinctively raised an arm to cover his face. It was enough. Dallas aimed for Archie's arm and threw himself on top of the man, bringing him to the ground.

Juno returned and danced in crazy circles around the two, barking at a deafening volume.

Dallas used all his strength to slam Archie's knife hand into the ground, but the kid held fast. He dealt Dallas a blow with his free fist that got him in the back of the head, sending stars shooting across his vision. A flash of fire across his forearm rocked Dallas back as Archie rolled away. Dallas scrambled to his feet, a line of red dripping from the wound on his arm.

Archie was already standing, eyeing the dog who continued to bark, uncertain, taking darting hops toward Archie and Dallas. "What happened to fetch?"

"He fetches people, not sticks, and he's not an attack dog, so don't hurt him."

"No," Archie said. "I guess I won't. Nice moves. Heard you were in a gang back in the day."

Dallas did not react to Archie's knowledge. Kid had done some research. "Not anymore."

"You can never get out of that world."

"Yes, you can. I did."

"You're gonna be in my face if I let you leave."

"If you're after Mia, then you're right. I will."

"Why? You into her or something?"

"Just a friend."

Archie gave him a look. "Uh-huh. Sure." He straightened. "Short on time, so I'm gonna end it here, but I'll take care of the dog for you."

"Appreciate that." Dallas went into a ready stance, learned not in a karate studio or a self-defense class, but from adrenaline-fueled fights with other lost young men bent on self-destruction. To defend their brotherhood, what had been his brotherhood, his family, or so he'd fooled himself into believing. All for Uncle, for the territory. He did not want to fight, but if it would free Mia, then he would do it. Juno whined, big torso heaving with confusion. A finder, not a fighter. Dallas wished he had spent his life doing the same.

Self-recrimination later, he told himself. There was no effective way to defend against a knife attack and he had the scars to prove it. Only one alternative that wouldn't get him killed and he took it. When Archie lunged forward, Dallas jerked aside and aimed a crushing kick at Archie's knee.

Archie's grunt of pain told Dallas he'd hit the target. He stumbled and Dallas aimed another kick at the knife hand which sent the switchblade spiraling into the bushes as Archie fell stomach-first onto the wet ground.

Dallas immediately knelt on his back, knee between the shoulder blades, shushing the furiously barking Juno.

Dallas's heart was pounding, the pulse hammering so loudly in his ears he did not at first hear the chug of a heavy vehicle approaching from the other side of the rock slide.

"Someone's coming. Moving fast," Archie puffed. "What are you gonna do? You don't move your truck, whoever that is could slam right into it and go over the cliff."

He was right, but the second he released Archie, the guy

would bolt or find his switchblade and have another go at Dallas. The pop of gravel sounded louder now.

No choice. He couldn't risk causing an accident.

He leaned closer to Archie. "Stay away from Mia."

Archie answered with a laugh. Dallas released his hold and ran to the truck, cranked the engine as Juno leapt in and got the truck out of the way with a screech of tires. He made it just far enough to pull off onto the narrow shoulder when Archie flashed by in his SUV, snapping off a salute to Dallas. A moment more passed before an emergency vehicle swept by, no sirens going, but lights flashing.

They, too, had to take the roundabout way to Mia's neighborhood since the main road was underwater. The driver gave Dallas a wave, thanking him for pulling off the road.

He settled in behind, trying not to crowd the responders. Should he worry more that the situation ahead had turned into an emergency? Or that he'd let Archie, the guy with a switchblade, get that much closer to Mia and Gracie?

Hands gripping the wheel, Mia answered Gracie's myriad questions mechanically, not realizing what she was agreeing to.

"I can have ice cream for breakfast? Super duper," Gracie said. "You never let me have that before. Not even Tina lets me have ice cream for breakfast, only cookies."

Mia blinked. "What? No of course you can't have ice cream for breakfast. I was thinking about something else, and Tina should not give you cookies for breakfast, either."

In truth, she was trying to squash down the concern that washed through her belly. Dallas had taken off after a stranger to do what? Confront him? Follow the car? She hit the brakes as a roadblock appeared. A police volunteer in an orange vest approached her open window.

"What is it? What's going on?"

"Levee failed. Town's flooded. We're evacuating now."

"But I've got to get to my house. I need to…" Retrieve a picture of a woman who was at the scene of a murder? That seemed too fantastic a tale to drop on the harried-looking volunteer who was already wet to the skin, though it had stopped raining. "I have to get something. It's important."

"Sorry, ma'am. It's not safe to drive in. You can see from the road there, where everyone is gathered. No farther than that."

She dutifully pulled the car off the road, turned off the engine and helped Gracie out. They skirted giant puddles and slogged through patches of grass until they came to a gathering of a half dozen people wearing emergency vests who were peering at clipboards along with the volunteer firefighters. It was a sort of makeshift emergency center with a pop-up canopy to keep off the rain. With Gracie bundled close, Mia drew to the edge of the bluff, gazing down at what had been her home.

The house she rented was one of only a half dozen, scattered in between with thickly clustered trees. Now the quiet, country road was a river, water lapping the middle of the doorways. At first she couldn't locate her house, until she saw the weathervane turning lazily in the breeze.

Gracie pulled at her mother's hand. "Where's our house?"

Mia breathed out a long sigh. She had not yet even managed to tell Gracie the hard truth about Cora, but there was no way to shield her child from this. "The levee couldn't hold all the water. It spilled over and flooded our house."

They stood for a moment in silence.

"When will the water go away?"

Great question, and she'd give her eye teeth to know the answer. "I'm not sure."

And when the water did recede, what would be left behind? Sodden clothes, ruined furniture acquired a bit at a time on her meager salary. And the rocking chair, oh that precious wooden chair snatched up at a garage sale when she shouldn't have spent the money. How many hours had she spent in that chair after Gracie went to sleep, studying her nursing coursework, dreaming about the future she imagined she was providing for her daughter.

A lump formed in her throat.

"Where are we gonna sleep, Mommy?"

The question danced away, unanswered on the wind. They watched an inflatable Zodiac boat, guided by two firefighters, as it approached the bluff carrying an elderly couple swaddled in life jackets, their sparse white hair pasted in wet clumps to their foreheads. She searched the area for Dallas. What had happened to him?

Mia felt a hand on her shoulder.

She turned to find Dr. Elias wearing an orange vest over a long-sleeved denim shirt and jeans. Her mind was still dealing with the shock of seeing her whole life submerged and she wasn't sure what feeling floated to the top at the sight of her former employer.

"I'm sorry," he said, eyes somber. "The Army Corps of Engineers couldn't save the levee. They tried their best."

Mia nodded. "I'm sure they did."

"Hiya, Dr. Elias," Gracie said.

He smiled and knelt in front of her. "Well, hello there. I'm glad to see you."

"Our house is all watery now."

"Don't worry, honey. We'll find you a place to live."

Mia took Gracie's hand. "The doctor is here to help people who are hurt. Let him do his job now."

Dr. Elias straightened and put an arm around Mia's shoulders. "Really, I can help you find a place."

She didn't move, torn between shock and uncertainty. Was this the man whom she'd thought meant to harm her only days before? There was no longer a clear answer to any issue crowding her mind and heart.

Where would they go? She had maybe twenty dollars in her purse and a credit card on which she'd already charged a semester's tuition. "Why would you want to do that after you fired me?"

He sighed. "I told you I would help you, even if you couldn't work at the clinic. You lied to protect your child, not to hurt me. I'm sensitive about lying. A foible of mine."

How had the talk become about him?

He squeezed her shoulders. "I can fix you up in…"

A woman approached, dark hair cut into a stylish bob that remained neatly coiffed in spite of the elements. The fragrance of a floral perfume clung to her, odd and out of place at a disaster scene. Green eyes flashed under delicate brows. "Thomas, you're needed at the launch point. They're going out on a rescue for a possible heart attack in progress."

"Of course." He patted Gracie on the head and jogged toward the Zodiac that was being readied to embark on the rescue mission.

The woman gave Mia a tight smile. Her face was carefully made up to show her fortysomething years to full advantage, jewelry small and tasteful. "I'm Catherine Elias, the good doctor's wife."

The slight sarcasm left Mia off balance. "I'm Mia Verde and this is Gracie, my daughter. I work… I worked for your husband until just recently. We met at a party you were kind enough to host for the staff." Mia's eyes were drawn again toward the water. "That was my house down there."

Catherine's face softened, giving her a more youthful look. "I'm sorry. This must be hard for you. No job, no house and a daughter to care for." She seemed to consider for a moment. "I heard Thomas telling you he could help you find a place and I guess…" She shrugged. "Never mind. I'm tired, that's all. Our kids are almost finished with high school, but I remember how difficult it is when they're young. But sweet, too, those little ones." She looked wistfully at Gracie.

"Yes," Mia murmured, uncertain how to respond to the sudden change in mood.

"We have a small cabin up in the mountains here. It's remote, but you are welcome to stay there until you get another place."

"Thank you. That is incredibly kind of you, but we'll find something." Mia was amazed that her tone was calm and controlled. Inside, her gut churned like the gray water splashing against the bluff.

When? Where? And most of all how? She felt like dropping to her knees and praying, but she would not crumble. Not now. Not ever again. She would make a way, where there was none. "Where are the townspeople being evacuated to?"

Catherine pulled her gaze from Gracie. "The college gym just up the hill. It will work for a night or two anyway. You can walk up, or there's a van arriving in a minute to carry people."

"Great." Mia scooped Gracie up. "Mommy always wanted you to go to college. You'll be the first four-year-old attendee ever. We'll just wait with the gang until the van arrives."

Feeling Catherine's eyes following them, she hastened toward the wet neighbors gathered in a forlorn group under a sodden canopy. She texted Tina, relieved when the girl answered back.

College classes canceled. Gone home to folks until flood's past. Kiss Gracie for me and try to stay dry.

"Hiya, Dallas," Gracie called over her shoulder.

Mia whirled, her spirit rising at the sight of Dallas loping toward her with Juno at his heels.

He gave Gracie a tight smile and she immediately crouched to administer an ear rub to Juno. Mud streaked his shirt, and Mia's eyes traveled downward, caught by the circle of bloody gauze tied around his forearm.

Her stomach clenched. "The man in the car."

"I'm okay, but he got away." Dallas seemed to weigh something in his mind before he leaned close and spoke in a low murmur. "He's keeping tabs on you for his boss."

She forced out the question. "Who is his boss? Never mind. It's Hector, isn't it?" Bitterness rose in her throat like a bubbling acid. "He's got people watching my every move. He'll never let us build a life without him."

"I don't think that's it."

Wind slapped her hair into her face. "Who then? Who would bother?"

"People who think Hector passed something on to you."

"Passed what?"

He didn't answer. Instead he showed her the picture on his cell phone. "Recognize him?"

Everything went fuzzy. She inhaled deeply, trying to stem the whirling in her head. "It's the man who broke into my house. I can't understand this. What is happening to my life?"

He embraced her then, and she let him. His arms pressed away the panic, the fear that grew with every passing day. The heat of his skin melted some of the numbing cold that gripped her.

"I'm checking into it. I'll have more answers soon."

"I've been in Spanish Canyon for months. Why would he come here now? What am I going to do?"

His embrace tightened. "Come back to the trailer. I'll keep watch. He won't get close."

Protection. Strength. Safety. And a delicious sliver of fascination. Dallas Black made all those things erupt in her belly. She turned so her lips touched the smooth skin of his jaw. His dark hair cocooned her face against the warm hollow of his neck. How her body craved the comfort of his touch, her soul cried out to have a partner to help her through the flood that she knew was far from over.

But she'd had that perfect union before. A God-blessed marriage, or so she'd thought, until she finally saw Hector for what he was. Now "until death do us part" sounded more like a sentence than a comfort. Never again. Never.

She stepped back, sucking in a breath. "I'm going to the college. They've got an evacuation shelter set up there."

He frowned. "You want to go sleep on the gym floor where anyone can get at you and Gracie?"

She took Gracie's hand. "We'll be safe there."

"Safe?" His face was incredulous. "This guy Archie was ready to kill me to get to you."

"There are lots of people going. We'll never be alone."

The muscles of his jaw jumped. "Absolutely not."

She stiffened. "We'll be in a group all the time. Never alone. Besides, you don't make decisions for me."

"Somebody should, because you're letting what happened to you with Hector color your judgment."

Cheeks burning, her stomach tightened into an angry ball. "I'm doing what's best for Gracie."

"Are you?" He fisted his hands on his hips, and she saw fresh blood welling through the white gauze when his muscles flexed.

Am I? Suddenly she wondered, but she couldn't reverse course now. Right or wrong she had to call the shots for Gracie. Just her and no one else. "I'll return your phone as soon as I can."

She pulled Gracie along to the van that had just wheezed up the slope, not allowing herself to look back. She knew what was behind her anyway. A disappointed German shepherd.

And one very angry Dallas Black.

EIGHT

"What?" Dallas barked into the phone.

Farley whistled. "Bite my head off, why don't you? Got a burr under your backpack?"

"Sorry. Bad day." Too bad to try to explain to Farley. He molded his tone into something that might pass for civil. "Do you have anything for me?"

"Seven P. Finnigans in the vicinity. Sending you those addresses."

"Thanks."

"And the car was rented to an Archie Gonzales, from Miami."

Miami. Not a surprise. "Okay."

"One more thing, man. Norm, over at the rental car place. I know him, and he's a crusty old codger. He's got trackers on the rentals."

Dallas's nerves quickened. "Illegal, of course,"

"Of course, but he's in favor of slapping a nice hefty fee on the cars if they're taken out of state. Anyway, it was easy to hack into his tracking system."

"Do I want to know how you did that?"

"Probably not."

"What did you find out?"

"Most of his routes were routine, except one I found interesting. Guess who he's been to see recently?"

"Not in the mood for guessing games."

"Dr. Elias."

"That's not news. I think he's been at the clinic shadowing Mia."

"Not the clinic. Archie's been to the doctor's house."

His house? Dallas struggled to put it together and almost missed the finish.

"At 3:13 a.m."

Not the usual time for social calls. "Thanks, Farley. I owe you lunch."

"Yeah, and a vacation in Maui."

"We'll start with lunch."

"All right, cheapskate."

Dallas disconnected. The next call would be to Reuben and Antonia. There was no more room to keep secrets. Mia needed to know everything. He swallowed, picturing her maddeningly stubborn brown eyes, the need for independence burning as bright as the hurt. When she knew, she would hate him.

But at least she'd still be alive.

Dallas's arm throbbed. He strolled as casually as he could through the collection of hastily parked cars on the grassy shoulder of the road, leaving Juno in the truck to catch a nap. He realized he was grinding his teeth when he passed Mia's battered car. If she'd listen to reason…if she'd consider the smart choice.

Like you did? His conscience flipped through the myriad prideful mistakes he'd made. Rival gang members he'd fought, threatened. Store owners he'd intimidated. Petty theft he'd committed to prove himself to his ersatz family. His damaged body would always be a reminder of that disastrous past.

Most of his shame came when he remembered the way he'd coveted the looks he'd gotten from people, the respect he'd imagined in their eyes. Turns out it was not respect, but fear. He'd been too blinded to turn from the smothering blanket of gang life.

In spite of his brother Trey's tough love born of experience.

With no regard for his mother's pleading requests and avalanche of prayers.

It had taken waking up in the hospital with part of his spleen missing and his knee on fire, shaking from alcohol withdrawal and his boyhood dream to become a Marine ruined, for him to fall on his face in front of the Lord. Maybe it was the humiliation of being handcuffed to the hospital bed, knowing he deserved to go to jail for many things, including possession of an illegal firearm and simple assault. Possibly it was the realization that he had shamed his mother, his brother and his father's memory. Undoubtedly, it was God shouting his name.

At rock bottom, there's no more room for pride.

Only God.

Once he'd let go, God had shown him the goodness in people, the desperate love of his family, his own potential to be a man who lifted others, rather than striking them down. Somewhere along the way, he'd found there was goodness inside him, as well.

The fall had hurt, and he wished he could help Mia learn what he had without the dramatic descent. He sighed. *God's job, Dallas. Yours is to keep her safe.* It was a good reminder. No matter what the oddball storm of feelings brewing inside, Mia was his job, his mission. In spite of the pain from Archie's knife, and Mia's ridiculous desire to stay at the college shelter, he moved on through the sea of parked cars.

He saw no sign of Archie's rental, a small mark in their favor.

Sunset was not due for another hour, but the clouds succeeded in sealing the light away behind a wall of gray. Bad sign. The levees were similarly stressed all over Spanish Canyon and the rivers and catchments swollen to capacity. On an up note, the last weather report he'd heard called for only a mild rainfall in the next forty-eight hours. With that weather break, they might be able to stave off any more serious flooding and evacuations.

The flood lent strange odors to the air—the scent of wet stone, sodden foliage and trees uprooted from centuries of packed earth. Mia's house was underwater to the eaves, and so was the picture that might shed some light on Cora's death. He guessed Archie had not been there in Mia's house looking for the photo, but searching for Garza's money. However the meeting between Elias and Archie still puzzled him.

He was about to return to his truck, parked well away from the others when a stealthy movement caught his attention. Trick of the cascading shadows? No, there was another pulse of motion near a well-appointed blue BMW.

He drew back, crouching behind Mia's car to watch as a slight figure stealthily opened the passenger door. Whoever it was wore a hat and a dark windbreaker. Pretty low for someone to take advantage of a disaster situation to rifle through someone's car. But it was true that disasters brought out both the best and worst in people. He was about to demand an explanation, when he realized this wasn't a stranger, not a total stranger anyway.

Easing closer, he could see Susan's profile well enough to be sure it was her, the red-haired woman who'd shown up at his trailer.

And snuck out with your knife, he reminded himself.

Still keeping low between vehicles, he crept nearer.

She sat in the passenger seat of the car, examining the pile of papers in her lap that she'd taken out of the glove box. So intent was she on her mission, she didn't look up until he wrenched open the door.

With a scream she bolted out, spilling the papers on the muddy ground. For a moment, she stood frozen, staring, chest heaving with panic.

"Breaking-and-entering a specialty of yours?"

She let out a gust of air. "The door was open. That's not breaking in."

"Whose car?"

Still no response. Keeping her in his peripheral vision he picked up one of the papers. Catherine Elias. "Why are you interested in Dr. Elias's wife?"

"She's a fake."

"A fake what?"

"She's living a lie, and I'm going to prove it."

"I thought you were interested in finding out who killed Cora."

She nodded, lips tight, eyes flat and hard as wet stones. "That's right."

"Do you think Catherine killed Cora?"

"Leave me alone, Dallas. This doesn't concern you right now."

He took a step toward her. "You're coming with me to the police. No more sneaking around breaking into cars. I'm out of patience with these guessing games."

She shook her head. "I'm not going with you anywhere."

He did not want to force a woman to do anything against her wishes, but this particular woman was dangerous. He took her wrist, the tendons standing out against the skin, pulse slamming violently through her veins. "You need to come with me, Susan."

He'd prepared himself for her to pull away. Instead she surged close, her clawed fingers pinching his biceps, face so close her sour breath bathed his face. "Listen to me," she hissed. "There are dangerous people in this town, people who are not who they appear to be." Her mouth twitched at the corners, and he fought the urge to recoil.

"Like Mrs. Elias?"

She did not seem to hear him. "Dangerous people who will kill Mia Verde and her little girl, just like they killed Cora. If you try to go to the police, or anyone else, they'll just kill her quicker."

His stomach flipped. "Who? Tell me, and I'll help you."

She moved back slightly to search his eyes. "Ah, sweet boy. Are you going to protect me from a killer?"

"If I can."

"I'm not afraid to die," she said, releasing his shoulders. "It's the living part that's scary."

He felt as though he was stuck in a strange horror film. Was she crazy? Was he, for letting go of her wrist?

The sound of voices made them both turn. Susan quickly returned the papers to the glove box and ducked down, yanking him to a crouch next to her. Through the window they saw Catherine Elias and an orange-vested volunteer consulting a clipboard as they walked toward the car. Catherine pointed to something on the first page and the two stopped to talk.

"Remember," Susan whispered, "if you tell anyone, Mia and Gracie will die. I'll contact you when I can." She sprinted off through the cars and ducked into a screen of trees. He scooted far enough away from Catherine's car that he would not be taken for a stalker, and then walked back to his truck where he sat on the front seat, brooding.

The obvious course of action was to go to the police, but they already suspected Mia of being involved in Cora's death. What would they make of his wild story about some mystery woman poking through Catherine's car?

Her words circled in his gut, cold and heavy. *"Dangerous people who will kill Mia Verde and her little girl, just like they killed Cora."*

Now his head pounded right along with the throbbing in his forearm. He should go home, back to the trailer to think it through, but he didn't want to be that far away from Mia and Gracie with Archie on the loose. If he checked himself in to the college evacuation center, Mia would be furious and possibly try to go find yet another unsuitable place to house herself and Gracie.

Juno poked his nose at Dallas, bringing him back. "What next?" his eyes inquired. The dog was eager to do just about anything Dallas requested except get his nails trimmed. That required several dozen treat bribes and some strong-arming from his owner. "Looks like we sleep in the truck again, boy, but I've got some kibble for you, don't worry."

He opened the door for the dog.

"Don't suppose you've got any notions on how to handle a stubborn woman, do you, Juno?"

Juno huffed out a breath and laid his head on his paws.

"Yeah, that's what I thought," Dallas said, giving his friend a pat.

Mia took the blankets offered to her and found her way to the side of the gym designated for women. She chose two cots together, but at a bit of a distance from the nearby family consisting of a wife and three teenage girls and a few older women who had already set up their makeshift beds. The two older women sat together, hands clasped, praying softly, one with wispy white hair. Perhaps they were sisters. Longing surged through her and she wished Antonia was there.

Gracie stared. "Is that Miss Cora? I want to go see her."

A pain stabbed deep inside. "No, honey. Just looks like her. The hair is the same color."

"Oh." Gracie said, looking up at the ceiling lights. "I don't like it here. Maybe we can go stay with Miss Cora. She prays nice, with songs and everything."

Tears collected in Mia's eyes, and she blinked hard. It

hadn't dawned on her until just then that she had never prayed with Gracie, that she'd funneled her own anger into a deluge that kept her daughter far from the Lord, too. Her choice had bled down to Gracie, staining her with Mia's own sin.

"Gracie, I'm sorry. Do...do you want to pray with me?"

Gracie nodded, grabbing Mia's hands. "Okay. I'll say it. I know how." Gracie thanked God for Mia and Cora and the cheese sandwich and cookies she'd gotten from the volunteer who'd included an extra sweet for the little girl and the blue blanket and Auntie Nia and Uncle BooBen. "And thanks for Dallas 'cuz he says Daddy can be good again and thanks for Juno 'cuz he plays with me. Ayyyyyy men!" The last word came out in such an unexpected volume that the others shot amused glances their way.

Mia raised an eyebrow. "That was a big amen."

"Cora says you should always fill up the amen with joy," Gracie said. "So can we go see her?"

That innocent heart had never confronted death before. Certainly Mia would never have chosen to tell Gracie in the wake of losing every possession to the cruel water that engulfed their house. This time, she did send up a prayer of her own, a halting, awkward, stumbling effort.

Help me tell her.

Help her cope.

Mia forced out the words. "Honey, I have something sad to tell you."

Gracie regarded her soberly, bouncing a bit on the cot beside her.

"Miss Cora died. I'm so sorry. Her house caught on fire and the smoke got inside her lungs." Mia watched in fear as Gracie's brow puckered. "She's in Heaven now."

"Oh." Gracie considered the news as a full fifteen seconds ticked away. "Can we stay at her house until she comes back?"

It was as if her heart shrank smaller and smaller, concentrating the pain until it nearly choked her. "She's not coming back, baby," Mia whispered.

"Never?"

Mia took Gracie's small fingers in her own. "No, honey. Never."

"Mommy, I think that's not right. She's gonna come soon. Can I keep the blanket?" Gracie held up the blue blanket neatly folded at the foot of the cot.

"Yes," Mia said weakly. "The volunteers said you could if you want to."

Gracie wrapped herself up and laid down on the cot, singing softly to herself.

Mia watched her, filled with a river of tenderness that almost overwhelmed her. It would sink in, in time, that Cora was gone. Maybe that was a gift God gave his little children, a gradual realization that was kinder, somehow than the swift bolt of knowledge. Shadows crept along the edges of the gym, and quiet conversations gave way to silence. Mia found she could not sleep, though the cot was not at all uncomfortable.

She tossed and turned on the prickly choices she had made, ignoring Dallas's advice. His words floated back through her memory.

"Ever hear that verse from Proverbs? Starts with 'trust in the Lord' and ends with 'Seek His will in all you do, and He will show you which path to take.'"

She yanked the covers up around her chin. He could afford to believe such things; he had no one depending on him except for a dog. Dallas would not wake up tomorrow to a hungry child with not a single spare pair of socks, no place to live and nowhere to go. That was going to be Mia's scenario in the morning and she'd have to figure out how to deal with it.

A gleam of light crept across the gym floor. Someone entered carrying an enormous pile of towels, heading after a moment of hesitation, toward the locker room. She sighed. At least there was the possibility of a hot shower in the morning. Again she tried to force her body to relax on the cot. This time her wandering attention was caught by whispered conversation as two people talked by the light of a battery-powered lantern.

Giving up the attempt at sleep, she got up in search of a drink of water and caught a sentence of the conversation going on near the doors.

"She's practically a stranger," a familiar voice growled.

"No, she's not," Catherine Elias hissed. "That redheaded wacko is stalking me."

Dr. Elias reached for his wife's hand, but she jerked it away, nearly upsetting the lantern. "She lost her husband. I treated her some time later. She attached herself to me and Peter."

"Peter Finnigan? You never mentioned that."

Peter Finnigan? Mia's heart beat faster at the name from Cora's email. She wanted to ask, to step forward into the lamplight, but she decided to retreat from the private conversation instead. As she did so, she heard Dr. Elias continue.

"I didn't want to upset you, honey."

"What's her fixation with me?"

He sighed. "She wants to be with me, ever since I treated her all those years back. I've tried to keep her away because she's…unhinged."

Unhinged. Mia crept back toward her cot, but not until she heard Mrs. Elias's reply.

"She's dangerous."

Dangerous. They had to be talking about Susan, the woman from the fire, who'd showed up at Dallas's trailer.

She was in such a state of confusion, at first she thought she'd gone to the wrong cot. "Gracie?" she called softy, turning in a quick circle.

Gracie's blanket lay on the floor, but the girl was no-where to be found. She'd gone to the bathroom. That was it.

Mia made her way quickly to the ladies' room. Empty. Jogging now back out into the main gym, she raced through the rows of cots, peering intently to see if Gracie had mistakenly crawled into the wrong bed.

There she was—at the end of the row, curled into a ball under the blanket. Mia felt the weight of the world rise off her shoulders and she heaved out a gusty sigh.

"You scared me, Gracie," she whispered, laying a hand on the girl's shoulder. "You're in the wrong bed."

The child sat up, blinking dark eyes. The woman on the cot reached out a protective hand. "This is my daughter, Evelyn. Can I help you?"

Shock rippled through Mia. Gracie was gone.

NINE

Gracie's here somewhere. She's not gone. Mia began to run now, around the perimeter of the gym to the men's area, in case her daughter had gotten confused. She rechecked Gracie's cot, snatching up the blue blanket to prove to her hands what her eyes could not accept.

Gracie was not there.

"Gracie?" What started out as a whisper, grew in volume until people began to sit up on their cots.

Dr. Elias and his wife materialized, lantern in hand. "What's wrong?" the doctor asked.

"Gracie's gone."

Catherine scanned the room. "I'm sure she's here somewhere."

Fear clawed at Mia's insides, prickling her in cold waves of goose bumps. "What if she wandered outside?" Down the hill, to the edge of the bluff where there was six feet of floodwater to fall into?

"We'll look right now," Dr. Elias said, heading for the door. "Catherine, keep searching inside." He put a hand on Mia's shoulder. "We'll find her."

At the moment, all her anger at the doctor dissipated in a cloud of hope.

We'll find her.

They ran outside, sprinting along the path to the edge of

the bluff, looking down into the swirling, moonlit water. Mia's stomach was twisted into a knot. Would she see her little girl floating there, facedown in the merciless waves? Shaking all over she forced herself to look.

"No sign of her. I'll look downstream," Dr. Elias said, handing her a flashlight. "Would she have gone to the woods back up by the gym?"

"I don't know," Mia answered. "I'll check there." She turned toward the patch of trees, dark silhouettes against the sky. Why would she head out of the gym on her own? Gracie was not afraid of the dark, but she did sleepwalk sometimes. Mia looked for signs that Gracie had passed by, but the ground was littered with bushels of fallen leaves and downed branches. The darkness wasn't helping, either.

"Gracie?" Mia called, her voice tremulous.

She walked under the dripping canopy. Droplets landed on her face like tears. "Gracie?" she called again. There was no answer but the rustle of pine needles, the movement caught by her flashlight the result of debris blowing along the ground. Gracie wasn't here, Mia could feel it.

She had to be inside the gym, she'd fallen asleep somewhere or gone to look for a snack. Mia was beaming the flashlight ahead to find her way out, when a man grabbed her from behind. A hand, smelling of nicotine, covered her mouth, as a strong pair of arms held her in a tight clinch.

"Mrs. Sandoval, listen carefully because I'm not the patient type and I want to go back to Florida. We know Hector has sent you a stash of money and it belongs to my boss. He wants it back. I've already searched your home and followed you around like a tracking dog, and I'm sick of it so I decided we should have a little meeting. Now, I'm going to move my hand so you can tell me what I want to know. If you scream, I'll hurt you. Understand?"

Blood rushing in her ears, she managed a nod. He peeled away his fingers and she turned to face him. It was the same man who had tried to trap them in her garage. She didn't care. There was only one thing her mind screamed out to know.

"Did you take my daughter?"

Archie's expression was hard to read. "I asked you a question. Answer."

"I don't have any money from Hector, and I don't know where it is."

"Mr. Garza thinks otherwise."

Garza. Powerful. Ruthless. A man who ran the Miami drug trade. "I don't have it. If I did, would I be renting a house here? Driving a secondhand car?"

Archie shrugged. "Not my job to figure you out, just to return the money. Got a tip that you've hidden it somewhere."

"A tip from whom?"

He didn't answer.

"Please," she whispered. "Did you do something to Gracie?"

Flashlights played over the grass outside the gym. Archie stepped back into the shadows. "Think about what's important and what you will lose if you don't give me what I want."

He melted away into the wet trees.

She ran blindly, branches slapping at her face, back toward the gym.

Gracie, Gracie, her heart chanted as she sprinted straight into Dallas, rocking back off his hard chest.

"Gracie's gone. Archie got hold of me."

His fingers dug into her shoulders. "Did he hurt you?"

"No."

His eyes dropped to her hands. "Is it hers?"

"What?" She realized through her fog that she was still holding the blue blanket. "This? Yes, it's Gracie's."

He called Juno and held out the blanket to the dog. "Find."

Juno bounded over the grass, startling those doing the flashlight search.

"Can he smell her?" she whispered.

"He's air scenting, following her smell." They watched the dog jog up to the gym entrance, scratching to be let in.

Dallas eased the doors open and Juno disappeared inside. Mia and Dallas followed her in. The dog followed the scent to the girl's bathroom, but stopped before he made it to the threshold. Juno circled a few times and stood, nose twitching.

Mia pressed shaking fingers to her mouth. "He doesn't know where she is."

"Give him a minute. There are a lot of scents in here. He's an older dog, so he's better at thinking it out and taking his time."

"Are you sure?"

"Trust the dog."

Trust a dog? With her baby's life? She wanted to yell, to scream at the top of her lungs as she watched Juno make a slow perusal of the room. Most of the occupants were awake now, helping look under cots and in corners, while others stood on the sides of the gym, giving Mia looks of abject pity.

She felt Dallas's hand take her hand and he squeezed hard. She clung to that touch as if it were the only thing that could keep her alive. Maybe it was. If Juno didn't find Gracie... She could not breathe, her ears rang.

She felt the room spinning, and Dallas forced her into a chair. "Deep breaths."

Waves of nausea and panic alternated through her body as she struggled not to black out.

Juno scratched at a darkened door in the back of the gym that Mia had not noticed.

"Stay here," Dallas said. "I'll check it out."

No way. Mia struggled to her feet, shoving down the dizziness by sheer willpower and staggered after him.

The exit opened onto a chilly hallway with metal doors at even intervals. Juno charged into the inky darkness.

Dr. Elias trotted behind them. "All the doors along this corridor are locked except the far exit door, for safety's sake. I saw to it myself."

"And the exit door? Where does it open?"

"Onto the parking lot," Elias said.

Mia ran to the end, ignoring the men. She was about to plunge through.

"Wait," Dallas said. He nodded at Juno who was pacing the corridor in regular arcs, nose quivering.

"You stay with your dog. I'm going to find my kid," Mia snapped.

"We might be wasting time," Dallas said. "Let the dog work, just for a minute longer."

"I don't have a minute," she shrieked. "Gracie might be out there in the water."

"This is why we train rescue dogs, Mia," Dallas barked. "They save time and effort and find a victim faster than a person ever could. You've got to trust the dog. Trust me."

For a long moment she stared at him. Seconds passed into excruciating minutes. Trust. She could not give it to him, not now, not with Gracie's life at stake. She pressed on the panic bar, just as Juno scratched furiously at one of the doors. Dallas opened it.

"So much for locked. It's a door to the stairwell." He held it for Juno who raced away. In a matter of moments, the dog returned, sat rigidly at Dallas's feet and barked exactly two times.

"It leads to the roof, I think," Dr. Elias said, voice low and hushed. "How did she unlock the door? Could a little girl climb three stories all by herself in a darkened stair-well?"

Gracie could. Hope and fear clawed together in her throat and she pushed forward, but Dallas had already plunged through the door, long legs churning up the stairs leaving Mia racing to catch up.

Dallas reminded himself as he ran that Mia did not know Juno like he did. Trust a dog? With his life. If Juno alerted, he'd found Gracie all right. The question was, in what condition? He knew she hadn't unlocked the door that led to the stairwell by herself. Dallas did not allow himself to dwell further on the thought. Three flights at top speed, following the sound of Juno's nails clicking on the concrete until he got too far ahead for them to hear. When they reached the door to the roof, Juno was sitting, nose shoved to the gap under the threshold, tail wagging for all he was worth.

I know, buddy. You found her.

With adrenaline surging his gut, he threw open the door and half fell onto the rooftop, Mia and Elias right behind him.

"Gracie," Mia screamed. "Where are you?"

Juno had already disappeared around a utility enclo-sure. When they rounded the corner, he was licking the tears off Gracie's face. The girl was sitting in a little ball, sobbing and hiccupping all at the same time.

His own sigh of relief was drowned out by the wail that came from Mia as she threw herself on her daughter, add-ing her tears to the mix.

Dallas called Juno and gave him a thorough pet and scratch. "Good boy, Juno."

"That's an excellent dog," Dr. Elias said with a winded laugh.

"Yes, he's the best air scenter I've ever worked with."

"And to think he does it all for kibble." Dr. Elias stared at Gracie and Mia.

Dallas caught something in the doctor's tone. "He does it for the joy of the find."

"How do you know he'll come back to you?"

"He's trained that way."

Dr. Elias nodded thoughtfully. "Good investment. You make a nice wage for that kind of work?"

Dallas tried to keep the disgust out of his voice. "We're all volunteer."

He nodded as if he'd just figured out why Dallas wore beat-up jeans and drove a ten-year-old truck. "My son, Jake, always wanted a dog, but we never caved in to that desire. We bought him lacrosse gear instead. Now he's the best on his team."

Dallas figured a lacrosse stick was a pretty poor substitute for a dog, but he refrained from saying so. He waited for a few more moments while Mia held Gracie so tight the girl squirmed for breath.

"Why did you come up here?" Mia said, at last pulling Gracie to arm's length. "You could have fallen. Why did you do such a dangerous thing?"

"It was dark and I was going to find the bathroom. A man told me they were closed and I had to go upstairs. He opened the door for me with a funny stick thing that he stuck in the lock."

"What man?" Dallas said.

Gracie shrugged. "I don't know. It was dark and he had a hat on."

Mia let out an exasperated sigh. "Why didn't you come back to ask me to go to the bathroom with you?"

"You weren't there."

Mia's face whirled through a storm of emotions before she settled on grabbing Gracie again and hugging her close. Over Gracie's shoulder she shot Dallas a look.

Dr. Elias reached for his phone. "I'm glad that's over."

"It's not over," Dallas snapped. "Someone sent Gracie up to the roof on purpose."

"For what purpose? To steal something while we were all busy searching? Mia and Gracie have nothing worth stealing." He looked thoughtfully at Mia. "Do you?"

Mia tightened her grip on Gracie. "No, we don't."

"I don't suppose it's…" He shot a look at Gracie and lowered his voice. "Someone who is reaching out from prison, for some reason?"

"Why would it be?" Dallas said.

The doctor shrugged. "True, I guess that's letting the past color the present. The door must not have been latched properly. Probably her imagination about the man." He chuckled. "My son was convinced for months that there was a bear living in our attic." He looked at Gracie, bending to look her in the eye. "I'm very happy that you are okay, Miss Gracie. I would be quite sad if anything happened to you." Dr. Elias dialed his cell phone to report that Gracie had been found. "I'll head downstairs and get everyone settled again."

He wiggled his fingers at Gracie and departed.

Dallas knelt next to the child, while Juno rolled over so Gracie could scratch the dog's belly. "Gracie, the man who told you to come up here. Do you think it could have been Dr. Elias?"

"No." She babbled to Juno. "You're a good doggie for finding me. I'm going to get you some Goldfish and we can share my blanket."

"How do you know?" Dallas continued. "How do you know it wasn't Dr. Elias?"

"'Cuz Dr. Elias smells nice."

"And the man who sent you up here didn't?"

"Nope," Gracie said. "He smelled like cigarettes."

Horror filtered past Mia's eyes as she squeezed her daughter closer. "Oh, Gracie."

"I told him cigarettes are bad." Gracie patted her mother's back. "He said to tell you something."

Mia tried to speak, but no sound emerged.

"What did he say?" Dallas used the calm tone he employed whenever Juno located a traumatized victim, the "everything is going to be absolutely fine now" tone.

"He said he was going to see us again real soon," she said.

TEN

Mia would not stay another second. Heedless of anything but the need to get Gracie out of that awful gym, she waved away the well-meaning urgings from Dr. Elias and Catherine to stay until morning.

"It's dark and the roads are treacherous," Dr. Elias said.

"Not as treacherous as staying here," she snapped.

"Someone phoned the police. They're sending someone, but it's not high on their list since Gracie's been located," Dallas said, grabbing the stuffed animal someone had given Gracie as Mia plopped her on the nearest empty cot to wrap her in a jacket.

"They can come find me if and when they send anyone." She pulled up the zipper. "We're not staying here."

Dallas did not ask where she was going. Honestly, she didn't have the foggiest notion, but Archie would not touch Gracie ever again and if he showed up, he'd wish he hadn't. Fury had replaced the fear. Anger was good, much better than helplessness.

Dr. Elias started to follow her as she led Gracie out the gym doors, but his wife stopped him with a whispered comment and a hand on his arm.

"Do you have my number at least?" the doctor said. "In case you decide you can't go it alone?"

Mia whirled to face him. "Thank you for everything, but that's exactly what I'm going to do."

Dallas followed her out. She hoisted Gracie on her hip and charged toward the makeshift parking lot, stopping short when she peered into the sodden interior of her damaged car. The rain had sheeted through the broken window and the seats were now sopping, bits of glass she had not seen before sparkling on the tattered vinyl.

One more thing. Another small obstacle, but it felt like the last tiny nudge toward complete desperation. She tried to keep her breathing steady as Gracie launched into a round of sleepy questions, rubbing her eyes with a fist. "Where will we sleep? I'm tired."

"Just a minute. Let mommy think." Could she get a ride? Borrow a car? Wait for the police and ask them to take her somewhere, anywhere?

An unusual detail caught her attention through the tension rippling her insides. Gracie's booster, still buckled in the backseat, had been covered up in a plastic garbage bag. She stared for a long moment before she turned around to face Dallas.

"Didn't want it to get wet," he said simply, hands in his jeans pockets. "Would have sealed the window, too, but I only had one bag."

The man had thought about something as menial and foreign to his world as a child's booster seat. "Dallas," she said, but a thickening in her throat kept her mute. She reached out very slowly and pressed her palm to the side of his face. He gazed at her in silence. She searched for signs of pity or disgust in his expression. There was nothing there but compassion and worry. "I am pretty sure that was the nicest thing anybody has done for me in a very long time."

"You deserve nice things, and so does Gracie." He

stroked the back of her hand, tentatively, as if it were a bird that might fly away at any moment.

She reached up to press a kiss to his cheek, but his greater height caused it to land just below his jawline. The stubble on his chin tickled her lips. The pulse that revved up in his throat seemed to pass into her body, until her heart matched pace with his. "Thank you," she whispered.

He cleared his throat as she stepped away. "I know you don't want to come back to the trailer. I'll help you find another place in the morning, but we can't right now. It's all there is. It's all I have to offer."

He left the question unspoken. *Will you come with me?*

"Why," she whispered, giving words to the question she hadn't known boiled and bubbled in her broken soul, "is it so hard to do it on my own?"

A beam of moonlight caught his face, highlighting the strong chin, wide cheekbones and a boy-like vulnerability under the tough guy mask. "Maybe because you weren't meant to. No one is."

Mia sagged under the weight of the words and her daughter's limp form. Dallas stepped forward, taking Gracie from her. She fetched the booster and they made a quiet procession back to Dallas's truck.

She squeezed the booster into the backseat of the double cab, and Dallas put her in and secured the buckle.

Juno hopped in next to Gracie whose eyes were at half-mast, licking her when he thought Dallas was not looking. After what Juno had done, Mia would never discourage him from being near Gracie again.

Dallas opened the passenger door for Mia, his body close to hers, and she pressed herself into his arms. "I don't want this," she said into his chest, dizzy with the nearness of him and the relief that Gracie was safe. "I don't want to…need someone."

"I know," he said as he bent his head and kissed her.

Electric warmth circled through her and pushed back a tiny corner of fear as her lips touched his. Breathless, she pulled away. "I should have said it sooner, but thank you for finding my daughter."

Eyes wide, he offered a tentative smile. "Juno found her."

"I'll pay him in Goldfish," she said, her own voice tremulous as she chided herself mentally. "But I don't know how to repay you."

"There's no debt."

The softness in his eyes brought her back to the heady emotion of that kiss. She almost lost herself in the feeling again before she snapped herself back to reality. His kiss was just a physical expression of what they'd just been through. *Don't feel for him. Don't love him.* Deep breaths helped her stop the wild firing of her nerves as he shut the door and went around to the driver's side.

The first ten miles passed in silence until Dallas told her about Susan.

Mia gaped. "Is she crazy? Making it all up?"

"I don't know."

"I heard Catherine say she was basically stalking him. She couldn't get over her husband's death and she became fixated on the doctor after he treated her. They mentioned Finnigan's name, too."

They mulled over the situation for the next half hour. Dallas edged the truck past a monster puddle that nearly swallowed the road. "I don't know who is telling the truth, but maybe this Finnigan is the place to start since his name has come up a few times now."

"Should we tell the police?"

"That's the million dollar question." He shot her a glance, dark eyes unreadable. "Your call." They made the final turn into the trailer park. "But you'd better decide now," he said as Detective Stiving emerged from the police car parked in front of Dallas's unit.

* * *

Dallas tried to hide his dismay that it was Stiving and not Chief Holder who greeted them. He lifted the sleeping Gracie from the back and handed her to Mia. Stiving let Mia get Gracie settled inside, Juno flopped down on the floor next to her. He stood on the front porch with Dallas until Mia joined them, a blanket wrapped around her shoulders.

"Folks told me you left the college gym. Said something unpleasant happened. How about filling me in?" Stiving took careful notes about Gracie's disappearance and the encounter with Archie in the woods. Dallas waited to see if she would reveal what Susan said, but she did not, nor did she mention Peter Finnigan's name.

Stiving arched an eyebrow. "So the Archic guy from Miami. He thinks you've got money from your husband squirreled away somewhere?"

Mia nodded wearily.

"Is he right?"

"No," Mia snapped, "as I explained to him. I'm a single mother with next to nothing in my wallet, no house, a ruined car and only the clothes on my back. I don't even have a change of clothes for Gracie. That's it. And even if I got Hector's money, I'd send it back express mail because I don't want anything to do with my ex-husband, thank you very much." The last few words came out a near shout.

Dallas could not have been more proud. After all she'd been through, she would not be steamrolled.

To Dallas's surprise, Stiving smiled. "Got it. Archie from Miami is a misguided individual. Targeting you for no reason."

Mia let out a squeak. "Does it matter the reason? He sent my child up onto the roof. He could have…hurt her."

"And no one else saw the guy?"

"I did, earlier," Dallas said.

"You don't count," Stiving said without looking at Dallas. "But adding a menacing stranger isn't going to throw me off the trail of who killed Cora."

"Incredible," Mia huffed. "What kind of woman would I be to use my daughter to deflect suspicion from myself?"

"The kind of woman that married a drug dealer and lived in the lap of luxury until hubby went to prison."

Mia's face blanched and she took a step back. "You don't know anything about me."

"I know more than you think. Fire Marshal says the house burned due to a candle fire, so that we have to rule as accidental, but the toxicology reports are what I'm eagerly awaiting. That's going to make for some interesting reading."

"I would never poison anyone, especially Cora," Mia said, arms folded tight across her chest.

"You stabbed a man before. Poison, knife." He shrugged. "Both can be lethal."

Dallas stiffened. "Knock it off. She doesn't deserve that."

Stiving looked close at Mia. "How do you know what she deserves?"

Mia sucked in a breath, then without another word she slammed back inside the trailer, leaving Dallas and Stiving alone on the porch.

"That was low. She's a good mother, the best," Dallas snarled.

"Really? You sound so protective. Good friend?" He quirked an eyebrow. "Or more?"

He burned inside. "None of your business."

"Let's lay it out here, Mr. Black. You and I don't get along."

"No kidding. Because I made you look bad by doing your job for you? Finding the kid when you didn't think it was worth your time?"

The smile vanished. "No, because you're a hotshot who makes trouble in my town. Whatever you think of me, I'm a good cop. Thorough."

"So do your job and investigate. You'll see she's telling the truth."

"Could be, but I think it's more likely that your friend Mia Sandoval murdered Cora and when the lab tests come back and prove that the pills were doctored with poison, I'm going to arrest her. As far as this Archie from Miami thing goes, if he really is threatening her, it's just deserts."

"Just?" Dallas spoke through gritted teeth.

"Sure. She's experiencing the fallout of being married to a mobster. She probably had full knowledge of Hector's activities the whole time."

"You're wrong."

"Maybe, but I'm right about the murder and you'd better believe I'm going to look real carefully at you, too, since you're so tight with Miss Sandoval and everything." He grinned. "Gang boy like you? Arrest record and the whole nine yards? Real stand-up guy."

Dallas bit back his response. It wouldn't help Mia to shoot off his mouth. It probably hadn't helped her that her supposed protector was an enemy of the town's police detective.

"I'll be seeing you around soon," Stiving said as he walked down the steps.

Dallas felt a desperate need to act, to take some small step that would help shed some light. He took a shot. "Do you know a Peter Finnigan?"

Stiving stopped. "Finnigan? Why?"

"Do you know him?"

Eyebrows drawn together, Stiving chewed his lip before answering. "Guy of that name lives about an hour from here in Mountain Grove. Used to live in California until he bought a real nice cabin here in Colorado."

"Know him personally?"

"Read about him." He shook his head. "Witness in a case a colleague of mine worked on in California decades ago. Surprised I remembered it."

"What kind of case?"

"Why do you want to know?"

"Why did it stick in your memory? A case that wasn't even in your state?"

His eyes narrowed to slits. "This colleague talked it over with me. He thought something smelled funny about the story. Just like something smells funny about this one. So you're not going to tell me why you're interested in Peter Finnigan?"

Dallas remained silent. He was not going to get anything more and he wondered if he'd blown it by bringing Peter's name into the mess. Besides, he needed to check on Mia. Now.

Stiving started up the engine, still smiling, and Dallas tapped on the trailer door before letting himself in. Mia sat at the little table, elbows propped on the surface. He tried to read her expression. Angry? Wounded?

"Sit down and quit staring at me," she said.

Angry. Good. "Stiving has no sense. Ignore him. He did give me a tip on Peter Finnigan in spite of himself. I've got a town name to research."

She drummed fingers on the table. "He truly believes I am a murderer."

"Cops are like that. Don't trust anyone. Don't take it to heart."

"Easy for you to say. He doesn't think you killed Cora." She shot a hasty look at Gracie who slept peacefully. She stared at the little girl, face softening until it was so tender he had to look away.

"Dallas, you…you don't think I would ever put Gracie

in danger on purpose, do you?" She turned those luminous eyes on him, and suddenly breathing was difficult.

"No."

"But what if I do it unintentionally? Trying to make a life here has only gotten us in trouble."

"Not your fault."

"I'm not so sure. My number-one priority is to give her a good life, you know?"

He nodded.

"But I look back over my life, and I can't believe some of the things I've done." She looked at her hands. "I stabbed my husband. I actually did that."

"You thought he was going to kill you and take Gracie, didn't you?"

Her sigh was miserable. "But I never imagined I could do such a thing—that I was capable."

It cut at him to see the self-doubt. "You were protecting yourself and your daughter. Don't let guilt twist it around."

She beamed a smile at him that lit up even the farthest corners of the trailer. He could have been sitting in a glorious cathedral and there would be nothing to rival the beauty he experienced at that moment, sitting in a trailer parked on the edge of a flood-threatened town.

"I appreciate your friendship," she said, "I really do, even if I haven't shown it. It's been a long time since I could trust someone."

Trust. The word fell hard on his heart. *But I haven't told you the truth, Mia. Not all of it.* He opened his mouth to let it spill. Tomorrow, everything would change because of the phone call he'd made outside that rain-soaked gym. He remembered the cascade of emotions she'd triggered in him with their kiss that seemed to live inside him long after her mouth was no longer pressed tight to his. Would it all be gone in the morning? Perhaps it was for the best.

She needed a friend, not anything more. He would be lucky if she still counted him in that circle after tomorrow.

"What is it?" Mia said, squeezing his fingers. She looked so tired, circles smudging her eyes. He could give her one night of rest, of peace, before her world turned upside down and his did, too.

"Nothing. Get some sleep. We'll talk later."

She laughed softly. "'Oh, I've got miles to go before I sleep.'"

He found himself smiling back. "Robert Frost. You listened in poetry class, too."

"Yes, I did." She pressed the laptop to life. "And I'm going to dig up some dirt on a certain P. Finnigan before I turn in."

He understood. She needed to do something, to manage one small element in a life that was spiraling out of control. "How about if I help?"

She slid over on the bench seat, and he settled next to her, his big shoulder pressed against her soft one, admiring her slender wrists as her fingers danced across the keyboard.

It took them two hours of following cyber bunny trails before they had the pertinent details.

Mia gathered her long hair to the side, eyes darting in thought. "So this Peter Finnigan was a dishwasher at a greasy spoon in Southern California. He's out walking one day and sees a man boating. The boater falls overboard and is caught up by a rip current and shouts for help. Finnigan tries to get to him, but is unable and fearing for his own safety he leaves the water and calls the authorities. By the time they show up, the man is swept away, body never recovered."

Dallas consulted the screen. "The drowned man is Asa Norton, a thirty-year-old small-business owner. He's presumed dead after the appropriate length of time. Survived by his wife—" Dallas leaned closer "—Susan Norton. There's a picture."

Mia crowded close, her cheek nearly touching his. It took everything in his possession not to turn his head and find those lips again. *Knock it off, Black.*

"Does she look familiar?" Mia breathed quicker. "Could that possibly be the red-haired Susan we know?"

"Could be, but it's a bad picture." He leaned away a little, to quiet the pulse rushing in his veins. He read on. "Susan received the ten million dollar insurance settlement for her husband's death." He scrolled down. "Nothing further about it."

Mia chewed her lip. "Something Cora knew about Finnigan troubled her. It has to be a clue as to who killed her, doesn't it?"

Dallas saw the kindling of hope in her eyes as if a light had been turned on inside, somewhere down deep. *Help me keep that hope alive, Lord.* "We'll find out." But would there still be a *we* tomorrow?

They were silent for a moment. Pine needles scuttled quietly along the trailer roof.

"Do you think Peter Finnigan has answers?" she said finally.

"Possibly, but it could also be dangerous to go track him down."

"Dangerous, how?"

"Take your pick. Floodwaters, Archie on the loose and Cora's murderer."

"Could Archie have done it? Poisoned Cora's pills?"

Dallas thought it over. "I don't see why he'd go to trouble. Let's say he suspected you'd left this treasure from Hector with her. He might have searched her house, but he could have done that while she was out. No need to bring attention to himself or the property by causing her death. He's here on Garza's behalf to retrieve Hector's stash, that's his priority."

Mia's breath caught. "But what if he was there searching for all this money he believes I have, and she stumbled across him?"

He saw where she was going. "Cora did not die because of you. Period."

"I wish I could be sure."

"I'll be sure for both of us." He got up from the table, put a hand on her shoulder, trapping some of her silken hair under his palm. Without stopping to think it out, he pressed a kiss to her temple.

She curled a hand up around his neck and held him there. He was certain at the moment, as the nerves tingled through his body, how blessed he was to know Mia Verde Sandoval. But there was a secret between them, a secret that would hurt her. Though it took every bit of will power he possessed, he pulled away. "You've got to get some sleep. Tomorrow will be a bear." *And I want to leave now, while you're still looking at me with that half smile on your lips and eyes that make my heart pound.*

"Okay," she said, a puzzled smile on her face. "Tomorrow has to be better than today."

He wished with everything inside him that it could be, but his brain knew differently.

"Good night, Mia. Sleep well."

He said good-night to Juno, made sure Mia locked the trailer door and settled into the old chair in his own unit, positioned to keep watch, the feel of that kiss still dancing on his lips. It was the last time he'd share a kiss with Mia. He pushed away the sadness and rustled up some grit. *Do the job, Dallas.*

If Archie came, he'd know it.

Protection was all he could give Mia.

And he'd give it with his dying breath.

ELEVEN

Mia awoke to the sound of sneezing sometime after eight o'clock. It took her a few moments of blurry-eyed confusion to figure out it was Gracie who lay in a tight ball on the bed. Juno poked his nose at her, tail wagging.

Mia padded over on bare feet across the sunlit linoleum. "Hey, baby. The rain stopped."

Gracie sniffed. "I gotta sore throat."

Pulling the covers back, she found Gracie pink-cheeked and nose running. "Uh-oh."

"I got germans?"

Mia laughed. "Germs. Yes, I think you're coming down with something." Her forehead felt warm under Mia's palm. She fetched a glass of water and encouraged Gracie to drink it. Fishing through her bedraggled purse, she was thrilled to find the slightly sticky bottle of grape flavored medicine purchased after Gracie's last go around with the "germans." Cora had tended to her through that illness, offering homemade chicken soup and plenty of read-aloud stories. Mia's throat thickened at the thought. In spite of the groans, Mia managed to get Gracie to swallow a dose of the medicine.

"I want my turtle slippers. Can we get 'em?"

"I'm sorry, sweetie. Your slippers are all wet at the house. I'll get you some more soon." Anxiety cramped her stomach as the worries attacked in full force. And how exactly would she get slippers, or Gracie's pajamas, let alone a house? Especially while evading a murder rap and a mobster who'd threatened a return visit?

We'll find Peter Finnigan, and he will have some answers, she told herself firmly.

She grabbed a pair of neatly folded socks that Dallas had left, along with a clean T-shirt. The socks went nearly to Gracie's thighs and they both laughed as she rolled them onto the child's skinny legs. Mia let her mind stray back to the kiss. Why had she allowed herself to be kissed, let alone to respond? She had no clue, other than it was the most amazing kiss she'd experienced in her whole life.

Juno shot to his feet and ran to the door. Mia froze, heart hammering, until there was a quiet knock followed by a familiar voice.

"It's Dallas. I've got some things for you."

Mia found that her spirits ticked up a notch as she went to the door, pulling fingers through her messy hair and straightening the big sweatshirt he'd loaned her before letting him in.

His dark brows rose at the sight of her. "I didn't know that sweatshirt could look so nice."

She blushed.

He held up a brown bag. "Trailer park manager gave me some clothes for you and some that might work for Gracie left over from her granddaughter's last visit. And guess what—" He shook a pink pastry box. "Anybody want doughnuts for breakfast instead of Goldfish?"

Gracie coughed. "Can't. I'm sick."

Dallas shot her a panicked look. "Sick? How sick?"

"Terrible sick," Gracie piped up, adding a cough on the end for good measure.

"Should we take her to the doctor? I'll get my keys." He turned to leave, but Mia grabbed his arm.

"Not that sick. Kids come down with things all the time. It's okay. I gave her some medicine. She'll be okay. I promise." Mia hid a smile at the uncertain look on his face. "Really, it's fine. Kids are tough."

"They are?" His lips quirked. "They're just so…small."

She took the pink box from his hands. "Gracie won't eat them, but I wouldn't want these doughnuts to go to waste."

Soon he'd brewed a pot of coffee and she'd devoured two sugar-glazed doughnuts down to the last crumb. Dallas sipped out of his mug, a look of amusement on his face.

She wiped her sticky fingers. "Don't you eat doughnuts?"

"No sweet tooth."

"You're missing out," she said with a sigh. "Doughnuts are nature's second most perfect food next to mac and cheese. I think they're even on the food pyramid."

"It was worth it to watch you enjoy them." He added in a low voice. "To see you smile."

She returned the grin. "You know, for a tough guy who lives with a dog, you've got a sweet side."

"Don't let it get around."

"Why? Are you afraid you might have girls pounding at your door? Surely there must be some woman who wants a chance to get to know the softer side of Dallas Black."

He flicked a glance out the window before he answered. "I don't usually let them get close."

"Why not?" She shouldn't pry, but for some reason it felt so natural to talk to him and she wanted to understand what made him tick, and why she could not get him out of her mind.

"Don't want to disappoint them, I guess."

"When the mistakes of your past come out?"

He sighed. "Something like that."

"It's funny. You're trying hard to keep moving, and I'm going crazy trying to put down roots."

Yet here they were, sitting in the same banged-up trailer

while a storm of trouble whirled around them. She watched the steam from the coffee drift past the waves in his hair. God had sent her a friend in Dallas Black, she realized. A friend when she most desperately needed one. But why did her feelings for him seem like something else?

He fidgeted with his coffee cup. "Mia, listen. I've got to tell you something and it won't wait anymore."

She felt a tremor inside. "Okay. I've had two doughnuts to shore up my spirit, and I don't see how things could get any worse than they were yesterday. Go for it."

Juno barked, and a second later they heard a car approach. Dallas peeked out the blinds.

Archie? The police? Her mind ran wild.

His expression was inexplicably sad as he went to open the door.

Mia blinked incredulously when her sister stepped inside.

"Antonia," she cried, wrapping her older sister in a massive hug. "Why are you here? How did you know where to find me?" She pulled her sister to arm's length. "Is everything okay? Is Reuben all right?"

Antonia chuckled. "I think I should be asking those kinds of questions." She looked over Mia's shoulder at Gracie. "Hey, Gracie girl. How's my niece?"

Gracie waggled her fingers and squealed. "Hiya, Auntie Nia. You're here. Where's Uncle BooBen?"

Gracie was perfectly capable of pronouncing Reuben's name, but her toddler nickname for him had stuck fast and it always made Reuben grin. Antonia kissed her. "I'll tell you in a minute. Let me talk to Mommy first, 'kay?"

"'Kay."

During the exchange, the flutter of unease in Mia's belly grew as she put some of the facts together. Dallas had not been at all surprised to see Antonia arrive. What's more, they seemed to be at ease with each other, as though they'd been in frequent contact.

The three moved away from Gracie. "What's going on?" Mia demanded.

Antonia squared her shoulders and kept her voice quiet. "First off, I'm here because Reuben and I love you and we're worried about you. We know Cora is dead and the police think it's foul play. We also know Archie is in town because Garza believes you've got Hector's jackpot somewhere. Reuben has gone to the prison to talk to Hector and tell him if there is such a prize, he has to fess up, because he's put you and Gracie in danger."

Mia held up a hand. "Antonia, how do you know all this?"

Antonia exchanged a worried look with Dallas. "Because Dallas has kept us informed. We hired him."

She could not believe she had heard correctly. "Hired?"

Dallas sighed. "They asked me to come to Spanish Canyon and keep an eye on you."

It took several tries before she managed a response. "What?"

"There were rumors that Garza's men were looking for something Hector had stashed," Antonia said. "Reuben and I feared they would come after you and Gracie."

The information landed like a bomb in her gut. "That's how you knew about Gracie climbing the tree. Your informant kept you apprised."

Dallas flushed.

"My fault," Antonia said. "I hounded him for details about Gracie. I shouldn't have, but I missed her so much."

Mia folded her arms, trying to steady her pounding pulse. There was more. She could see it in their faces. "What else?"

"Cora was an old friend of Reuben's mother," Antonia continued. "When we heard you were thinking of settling near here to go to school, we contacted her and she offered to help."

Help? Cora? The truth started to worm its way through Mia. "So Cora helped me get a job, find a house to rent. She made sure Dallas had work fixing her roof so he could spy on me. What an amazing network to put together a life for one helpless woman and her kid."

Antonia touched her arm, but she shook it off. "Mia, we knew you wouldn't accept any help because you're stubborn and desperate to prove you don't need anybody. I'm sorry. I didn't want to tell you like this, but that's the truth."

"You knew I wouldn't accept it, but you arranged it all anyway, didn't you? Totally against my wishes." Anger hummed through her veins. "All this, everything I thought I accomplished here, was just charity, set up by people I thought were my friends."

"I'd like to think I am your friend," Dallas said quietly, "no matter how it came to be."

Mia turned her eyes on him. "You don't *hire* friends." Each word fell out of her mouth, cutting like glass. She saw him flinch and she was glad.

Antonia's chin went up, as it had for every head-butting argument they engaged in over the years, from which breakfast cereal to eat to the dire consequence of dating Hector Sandoval. "Listen, Mia. I know you're mad at me and that's okay. I knew that was a price for trying to protect you, but Dallas isn't doing this for pay. As a matter of fact, he refused any compensation at all. He cares about you, like we do."

Cares about you. And lied just like Hector and her sister. She found it hard to breathe. "So, why exactly are you here now, Antonia? Dallas hasn't been feeding you enough information? You had to check up on me personally?"

"Dallas called us after Garza's man showed up at the

college. I came to try and convince you to come back to Florida with me, until the thing with Archie is resolved."

"Didn't your informant tell you I'm shortly to be accused of murder? I don't think I'll be able to leave even if I wanted to."

"We'll get a lawyer if it comes to that. Let's try to get you out while we can. It's safest for Gracie."

Mia exploded. "Don't tell me how to be a mother to Gracie, Antonia," she snarled. "That little girl is the only thing I've done right in my whole life. Please don't imply I've messed that up, too. I can't take it." Dismayed to find tears on her face, she dashed them away.

"I never would," Antonia said, eyes anguished. "Honey, you're a wonderful mother. You just need help right now. That's all."

The emotion on her sister's face, the moisture that shone in her eyes, was too much for Mia. The fire ebbed out of her body, leaving only a dark despair in its place. She sank down on the bench seat. Antonia was right. She could not make a life for herself and Gracie. She did not even realize that her whole world in Spanish Canyon was a setup, neatly arranged for a woman who could not manage on her own.

But Dallas… She could not even look at him. Everything she imagined he'd done for her out of kindness, or, she hardly dared admit it, love? It was a job. She was a job to him.

"I guess I'd better do what you say. I can't trust myself."

Dallas sat across from her. "Mia, you're stronger than anyone I know. What we did… It was only because you have too many powerful people working against you."

"No," she said, her own voice sounding strange and dull in her ears. "You did it because you and Antonia and Reuben all believe I could not manage my life on my own."

"No…" he started, reaching for her hands.

She would not touch him, not look at him. "I said 'All

right.'" She fought the thickness in her throat. "You're both right, and I'm not going to argue. When do we leave?"

"I'll get us a flight tonight," Antonia said.

"Tomorrow." Mia glanced toward the bed. "Gracie's sick, and there's something I need to do first."

Antonia quirked an eyebrow. "What? There's talk that the weather might turn bad again. I really think tonight is better."

Dallas stood, hands on his slim hips, eyebrows drawn together.

Mia stared at the pink doughnut box, incredulous that only moments before she'd wondered if her feelings for Dallas could be more than friendly. *They're right. You can't trust yourself.* Dr. Elias's words came back to her.

"...you're afraid that you can't trust yourself, your choices, your judgments." Even her former employer had been able to see her deepest fear that had now been proven true. But she would not walk away, not from the murder of an old woman who had been trying to help her purely out of kindness. She was not a coward, not yet. "I'm going to find Peter Finnigan. He may be able to shed some light on Cora's death."

"No way..." Antonia said.

Mia whacked her hand on the table, startling Juno. "No matter how it came to be, Cora was my friend and Gracie and I loved her. I have to at least try to find out if Finnigan knows something. Please allow me to do that. Will you stay with Gracie?"

Antonia chewed her lip. "Of course, but I don't think..."

"I'll go with Mia," Dallas said.

"You don't need to do that," Mia told him. "Your spy identity has been compromised."

He flinched as her arrow hit the mark. "I'll go."

She didn't argue. If she said no he would follow her anyway. It was his job, after all, she thought bitterly, and he would do it until she and Gracie boarded that plane to Florida the following day.

She knelt next to Gracie and smoothed her hair. "I'll be back soon."

"Mommy, are you mad at Auntie Nia?"

"No, honey. We just had a disagreement. Auntie's going to stay with you while I run an errand. Is that okay?"

"Yes. Will Juno stay?"

Dallas nodded. "I think that's best."

"When you come back are we going to Florida?"

Mia exhaled. "I think so, baby."

"Is that gonna be our home?"

Mia thought there was never such a perfect little face as that of her sweet girl, staring at her expectantly, trusting that no matter what, her mother would provide a home. Was Florida going to be that home? Would any place ever be?

"I'm not sure if we'll stay in Florida."

She sneezed. "Will Juno and Dallas come, too?"

She could not answer above the sudden wave of sadness.

"Hey, Goldfish girl," Dallas said. "You just work on getting better. We'll talk about it later."

"'Kay."

Dallas offered a hand to help Mia get to her feet. She pretended she didn't see. *I'm a job to you, Dallas. Let's keep it that way*, she thought over the grief washing through her body.

Dallas tried to open the door of the truck for Mia but she scooted around and got in herself before he had the chance. What had he expected? She believed he'd betrayed her—and maybe to a woman who so desperately craved independence, he had. He'd crossed many people in his life, disappointed dozens, notably himself, but what he'd done to Mia hurt her worse than any other offense he'd dished out. It had been wrong to deceive her, even though the reasons were right.

I'm sorry, Mia.

The distance between them seemed like miles instead of inches. She stared out the window as his tension grew.

Should he try small talk? Apologize again? Mention the haze of clouds that had started to gather along the sunlit horizon?

Talk about the weather? Stupid, Dallas.

He settled on silence, trying to ignore the leaden feeling in his limbs. He'd hoped in that idiot macho way of his the truth might blow over as the miles went by and he could start again, trying to show her how much she meant to him. Judging from the hard line of her mouth, he'd thought wrong. If only women were as forgiving as dogs.

"Why did you do it?"

He jerked a look at her, startled, praying he would not make it any worse with more idiotic conversation. "To protect you. At least that's what I thought I was trying to do."

"No, I mean why did you do it for nothing? Agree to take the job without pay."

Because to me, it's not a job. "Antonia asked me. I respect her and Reuben."

"You didn't move to a strange town because you respect my sister and brother-in-law."

He shifted, setting the seat springs squeaking. "I never care much where I am. One town is as good as another. Spanish Canyon offered a decent place to teach Search and Rescue classes. Why not?"

She turned gleaming brown eyes on him, skewering him to the seat back. "That's not it. You moved to this town, spent hours working on an old roof and living in a trailer, for no pay, to protect a woman you barely knew. Why did you do that? I think I deserve to hear the truth."

She did, but he knew it meant sharing messy, unformed

feelings, incoherent ramblings of his heart that he himself did not understand. He flipped through the memories that had swirled through his mind almost daily since he'd seen her in Florida following the hurricane. "At Antonia and Reuben's wedding. I saw you talking to Gracie before the ceremony."

She waited.

He sighed. "I dunno, something about what you said to her got inside me and stayed there."

"What did I say?"

He tried to repeat the words exactly. "Gracie was little then, just a toddler. Is that what you call that age?"

She nodded.

"Anyway, she asked you where her daddy was and you knelt down, right next to her and told her Daddy was in jail because he made mistakes."

He heard her sniff. "Yes. I remember now."

"And she started to cry so you said, 'We're going to be a family, you and me, and Mommy's going to make it all right.'"

Mia lowered her head. "I haven't made it anywhere near all right."

He went very still, the sound of the tires creating a soothing cadence. *Lord, help me to put words to the feelings, words she can understand.* "You were strong then, and gentle, too, just like you are now. I knew how hard it was going to be, with your past, and starting all over with a daughter and Hector's legacy. I understood because I have wreckage in my past, too." He reached out slowly, praying she would not jerk away from his touch, and covered her hand with his. "I wanted to help you and Gracie have a better shot at making a way for your family. That's why I told Antonia I'd do it."

She looked at their joined hands and one tear splashed onto their twined fingers.

"My whole life has been about where. Where will I go next. This time…" He struggled to find the words. "This time it was about the who, about you and Gracie. I wanted you to have a life." He swallowed hard. "And I guess maybe I wanted to be a part of that in some way."

It was too much. She pulled from him. "I didn't ask you. You invited yourself into our lives and you deceived me."

It cut at his heart. "I'm sorry."

She fished for a tissue in her pocket. "I understand your motives were sincere. Hector was sincere, too, but he did not trust me with the truth, either."

Her words stung like acid. He'd been put on the same shelf as Hector, a manipulator, a disappointment. Had he permanently severed that delicate strand between them? He could think of nothing to say to repair the break, not one word of comfort to bring the warmth back to her eyes.

The miles droned by in miserable silence until he turned on the weather station just to break the terrible quiet. It was not good news.

"More rain is on the way from an unexpected grouping of storms rolling in. A series of flash-flood warnings and advisories have been issued. Mudslides are already being reported near Mountain Grove and Coal Flats where rainfall on burn areas is causing ground failure. Residents are advised to be ready to evacuate."

Dallas took comfort in the fact that at least the trailer park was high enough to keep Antonia and Gracie safe. For a while.

"We should…"

She shook her head. "I'm going to see Finnigan. If you want to head back, just let me out."

Right. As if he would even consider leaving her on the side of a mountain road. Women. He wisely kept his thoughts to himself and pressed on at as quick a pace as he could manage. The steeper the grade, the more he began to worry about the possibility of mudslides. Slopes already sodden with moisture needed only a tiny push from nature and gravity to loosen tons of debris on the road below.

Finally, they turned off on an uneven path that took them through acreage so densely crowded with lodgepole pines that he thought Farley might have ferreted out the wrong address, until they came to the edge of a swollen river with a striking house set beside it. The dark wood tones and forest green roofing material made it appear as if the house was a part of the mountainside behind it.

They got out in time to receive the first drops of rainfall.

"Peter Finnigan has a nice little piece of real estate," Dallas said, perusing the boathouse that perched at the waterline and the modern shingled siding on the house above. "And he doesn't like being too close to the neighbors."

"He must have found something better paying than being a dishwasher." Mia started up the graveled path toward the house. As he followed, Dallas noted a green car parked behind the shrubbery, and the muscles in his stomach tightened. He put a hand on the hood. Still warm.

"Mia," he said.

There was the sudden sound of breaking glass followed by a shout.

Dallas took off for the house at a dead sprint.

TWELVE

Mia was gasping for breath by the time she made it to the house, pulling up next to Dallas who had just about reached the front door when it was flung open. A short, balding man stopped short, mouth wide. His arm was half raised, as if to shield himself from a blow.

"Peter Finnigan?" Dallas said.

The man glared, the fleshy pouches under his eyes bunching. "Who wants to know?"

"We heard a scream," Mia panted, by way of explanation. "Glass breaking."

"There's nothing wrong," he said. "Everything's fine. Go away."

"Not quite, Peter" came a singsong voice.

Mia gaped as Susan stepped up behind Peter. She wore clean clothes, her hair in a neat twist, a placid smile on her lips. Dallas seemed equally at a loss for words until he managed, "Are you hurt?"

Susan laughed. "Such a gentleman." She gave Mia a coy look. "You should keep him."

Mia's cheeks burned. "Susan, what's going on?"

She waved them in with an airy gesture. "Come in, why don't you? I just came to see Peter. We're acquainted. He's the man who tried to save my drowning husband, so he says."

Peter scanned the porch quickly, as if he was assessing the likelihood of an escape. Then he mumbled something, stepped aside and allowed them to enter.

"I'm glad you're here. She's some loony who busted in. When I wouldn't give her what she wanted, she started throwing things. I'm leaving just as soon as I can get her out."

Mia noticed a floral fragrance in the air and there was something familiar in the smell. Peter pulled keys and a wallet from a small bowl. While his back was turned, Mia spotted an old photo on the floor, partially hidden by shards of glass that littered the hardwood floor.

The snapshot was old and grainy, but it showed Peter with a taller man, heavily bearded, standing in a small boat. A third man was seated, holding a net. Peter stood to the left of them, dangling a fish for the camera, grinning.

She saw Susan looking at her. Quickly Mia tucked the picture into her pocket.

"What got smashed?" Mia asked.

Susan waved an impatient hand. "I startled Peter and he dropped his drinking glass. I was asking him what he knew about my husband's death."

He flashed a sullen look. "I dunno what you're talking about. She's crazy, like I said."

Susan sighed. "All right, I'll get the ball rolling. Let's stroll down memory lane. Fifteen years ago, you saw my husband, Asa, drown, didn't you? What a story you told the police about how you tried in vain to save him, battling the waves at your own peril. Made yourself look like a real hero."

Peter folded his arms, then unfolded them and shoved his hands in the pockets of his faded jeans. "You already know what happened, Susan."

"So," Susan said, her tone cheerful as if she was reciting a bit of poetry. "You lied. You and Thomas." She looked at

Mia and Dallas. "Dr. Elias, as you know him. To me he'll always be Thomas. Peter arranged with Thomas to make it look like an accidental death. Thomas was hoping to get his hands on the life insurance money. He pays you to keep quiet. That's how you afford this lovely home, isn't it?"

Peter grimaced. "You're nuts, and you're not telling the whole story."

"I probably am nuts. I've had a hard life after all. It took me a long time, years and years, to find Thomas and you. I tracked him down to Spanish Canyon. What a surprise to find out he'd started a whole new life here as a well-respected doctor. And you, too. Cora overheard Thomas threaten me at the clinic after I confronted him. She wanted to go to the police, but I told her they were on his side. She promised to help me find proof to take to the authorities."

"Cora?" Mia gasped. "Susan, tell us what happened."

Peter cut Mia off. "This is nuts. I'm not talking to any of you anymore. Get out, all of you."

Susan's face whitened and filled with hatred. "Thomas killed Cora because he knew she was looking into his past, and the truth was coming out. Now Thomas's going to have to eliminate anyone who can incriminate him and that means you."

"Are you insane? I've never caused him any trouble. I've kept my mouth shut about everything for all these years. He trusts me."

"Not anymore," she said quietly. "Not after he's had to murder again. This time he's going to button up all the loose ends."

Including Susan. Mia shuddered.

"Crazy, but I'm not gonna take the time to sort it out," Peter snapped, turning away. The back of his neck was red.

Mia's mind was still spinning, trying to put it all together. When Peter whirled back around, he held a gun snatched from his pocket.

Dallas stepped in front of Mia. "You don't need to do that, Peter. We're not here to cause trouble for you. We just wanted the truth."

"I'm getting out of this whole business. I was going to leave because of the flooding anyway, so I'll just make it permanent. If any of you tries to come at me, I'll kill you. I don't want to, but I will."

Susan chortled. "You can't get out. You'll never get out."

"Shut up," Peter barked. "Move away from the door."

Dallas and Mia edged aside. Mia took Susan's skinny wrist. "Let him go, Susan." Surprisingly, she did not resist.

"He won't get away," she said softly. "You'll never, ever get away."

Susan allowed Mia to guide her to the corner. When Peter fled out the door and down the path, Dallas ran to the window.

"He's got a boat ready." Dallas was dialing 911 as he watched. After a minute, he disconnected with an exasperated groan. "No signal."

Peter thundered down to the edge of the dock where a motorboat was moored. He cast off the lines and began to putter out into the swiftly moving water. A duffel bag in the back indicated his departure had been planned out.

Keeping low, Dallas sprinted toward the boathouse. He was going to see if there was another boat.

"Stay in the house," he yelled.

Mia watched as Peter piloted through the rough waters.

She and Susan edged out onto the porch. Mia could not stand it a moment longer.

"You have to tell us everything, Susan. We have to know who killed Cora."

Dallas vanished into the darkened interior of the boathouse, emerging a moment later with hands on hips. There was no other boat. Peter would get away and take his answers with him.

Dallas began to jog back to the dock. Mia started down the steps, leaving Susan behind. Thirty seconds passed. A flash of light and an earsplitting bang shook the boards under their feet. Mia's ears rang. Following Dallas's horrified gaze she realized the explosion had come from the boat.

Peter's duffel bag was burning, along with the interior of the vessel. Peter lay facedown in the water, his shirt on fire.

Susan stared, hands jammed into her pockets.

Dallas finished his sprint to the dock and jumped in the water, arms chopping through the waves. Bits of flaming debris sprinkled down around his head as he pressed on. It was a futile effort. By the time he'd cleaved through the swirling river to the spot where the boat had exploded, Peter's body had been sucked away by the current. The swollen river jerked and pulled at Peter, tumbling him along like a discarded doll. Dallas swam after Peter, and Mia found herself shouting, stomach twisted in fear.

"Dallas, come back. The water's too strong." *You'll drown,* her heart finished for her. She doubted he'd heard over the swirling cacophony, but he must have come to the same conclusion. She watched with her heart hammering at her ribs as he fought the water back toward the bank and Mia grasped his forearms to pull him from the river.

He stood, head bowed, water running from his hair and clothes. His broad shoulders drooped and quite suddenly, she wanted to comfort this man who had betrayed her. She raised her arms to embrace him. *Strength, not emotion, you ninny.*

Instead, she snatched up a towel that lay drying on the wooden rail and draped it around his shoulders. His eyes were shocked, horrified, drawn to the river where Peter Finnigan had just lost his life. In spite of herself, she pressed her hand to his biceps for a moment.

He imprisoned her palm there, his own fingers cold. "I couldn't get him."

She allowed the touch to linger before she pulled away. "No one could."

He heaved in a breath. "I'm guessing there was an explosive device in his duffel bag. It was motion triggered." He paused. "Or someone set it off by cell phone."

Mia glanced into the acres of dark trees and shivered. Were there eyes watching from the shadows? Eyes glowing with satisfaction at the death they had just witnessed? As they moved back toward the house, she realized Susan was still staring out at the burning boat, spinning in helpless circles as it moved downriver.

"I told you, Peter," she whispered.

Dallas left a trail of water along the floor as the three of them searched for a phone with a landline. Nothing. His own cell was now waterlogged thanks to his instinctive plunge into the river and there was no chance of getting a signal anyway. In the course of their hunting, thunderclouds began to roll in along the river canyon, obscuring the mountaintops under a blanket of grey.

"We need to get out of here," Dallas said. "We'll keep trying to call on your cell as we drive."

Mia patted the photo still tucked in her pocket. "Come on, Susan. You can fill us in on the way."

"My car is here," she said. "In the bushes."

"We'll bring you back for it later." Dallas was not about to let the woman slip out of their grasp again. Especially not after what had just happened to Finnigan. He still burned inside with the knowledge that he had not been strong enough or fast enough to pull the man from the monster river. An epic failure and a life lost. Trying to keep watch for any sign of movement from the tree line, they returned to the truck. He fought the urge to bundle both women back into the house and barricade them safely inside, but with floodwater rising all around them, it was not an option. "Let's move a little faster," he said, putting an encouraging palm on Susan's bony shoulders.

Back in the truck with Susan in the backseat, Mia didn't waste a moment.

"How did you know about Peter?"

Susan sighed. "I'm very tired." She leaned her head back on the seat.

"I'm sorry, Susan," Mia snapped. "But we just saw a man murdered back there. You need to start talking."

Dallas felt the tingle in his stomach at the strength in her tone, the fire in her words.

Susan sighed and tears welled up in her eyes. "I killed him."

Mia gasped.

Dallas gripped the wheel as Mia blinked in shock. "Who?" she managed.

"My husband, because I got involved with Thomas. He was a medical student, deep in school loans and credit card debt, but charming, and he seduced me. Made friends with Asa, or pretended to. He knew how unhappy I was in my marriage, but I never dreamed… How could I know Thomas would murder Asa? Actually murder him? I blame myself for Asa's death. I always will for bringing Thomas into our lives."

"You had no idea what kind of man he was?"

"None," she sniffed. "Thomas knew Asa had planned a fishing trip. Asa had a high-stress job running his own business, so fishing was his escape. I think Thomas drugged his bottle of tea so he became unconscious. Peter was waiting nearby, and he made sure Asa tumbled out of his boat and drowned and then he told the story of trying to save Asa so the police wouldn't look into it too closely."

"Dr. Elias did it, why? Out of jealousy? So you two could have a life together?"

Her voice hardened. "Nothing so romantic. Thomas knew Asa had a life insurance policy, and he figured after he killed Asa I would give him the money because we were, um, in love. At least I thought we were. Completely stupid of me, of course. Maybe Thomas figured once I received the payment he could kill me then, too."

What was one more murder for the guy? Dallas thought.

"When the insurance company signed off, I collected the money and ran as far and as fast as I could, but I always knew I'd make Thomas pay." An edge crept into her voice. "Thomas wanted to make a fresh start with a new identity, the good doctor beloved by all, but I found him. And Peter, too."

Dallas hit the brakes as a small pile of rocks showered down onto the road. He guided the truck around it, trying to process Susan's revelation.

"I confronted him, and Cora overheard and started checking into things. She told me she found a photo that she could use against Thomas, but before she could show me, she died. Thomas killed her, I'm sure of it." Dallas saw tears slide down her face. "He got himself a new life. And a pretty new woman."

He remembered finding Susan breaking into the BMW outside the makeshift evacuation center. "It's Catherine Elias, you've been following, isn't it?"

Mia jerked. "The floral perfume fragrance. I thought it was familiar. It's Catherine's. You followed her to Peter's?"

"I've been watching her house. I was curious to see if she knew what kind of man she was married to." Susan laughed. "She's scared of me. Anyway, she brought him the photo of Peter and Thomas. Don't know how she got her hands on it unless she was in on Cora's murder the whole time."

Mia took the photo from her pocket. "Who is the seated man in the boat?"

"Asa." She chewed her lip. "You see? Shows the three were acquainted, though Peter claimed to be a random stranger who saw Asa drowning. The photo proves a connection between them, and the police would connect the dots, I have no doubt."

"And why would Catherine take the photo to Peter? Blackmail? To set him up to be murdered?" Mia wondered aloud.

"Or she's innocent," Dallas said. "Could be she found the photo after Elias took it from Cora and she became suspicious, wanted to check up on her husband."

Mia slid the photo in the visor, staring at it as they drove.

Rain slammed into the windshield. Susan turned her face to the glass and watched the water sheeting along the window. Her eyes drooped. "I'm too tired to talk anymore."

He did not think Mia was even breathing until she heaved a long shaky breath. "It's true. Dr. Elias killed Cora."

"And Asa, and Peter," Dallas said.

"And he'll do the same to me, if he gets hold of me," Susan said.

"But now we have proof." Mia's voice held a tone of wonder. "We can go to the police and expose him. I can have my life back."

The hope shone on her face and his pulse trip hammered. Where would that life take her? Back to Florida? To some other faraway place? Didn't matter. Wherever it was, it wasn't going to include him. He cleared his throat. "Try the police again."

She did, with no better result.

They made it over the top of the mountain and began the descent. Half a mile later, he pulled the truck to a stop behind another truck and an SUV. A gnarled ponderosa pine had clawed free of the earth and fallen, blocking the road in both directions. The road was hemmed in by a steep drop on one side and the mountain on the other.

Dallas got out to talk to the bearded man from the truck just ahead of them. The guy was fetching a chain saw from the covered cab of his vehicle. He introduced himself as Mack.

"Gonna have to chop it up and haul it off as best we can," Mack shouted to Dallas over the roar of the chain saw. "Folks are gonna be packing this road to get out of here if the rain don't stop."

"How much time you figure before they order evacuations?" Dallas called.

"If the storm don't turn ASAP, they'll be evacuating before nightfall. Rivers are full."

Recalling Peter's body whirling away on the swollen river, Dallas fought a pang of horror. He started in, hauling away the branches as the bearded man cleaved them from the trunk. The two from the other stopped vehicle, a father and his strapping teen son, set to work helping also.

"Got some orange cones in my truck," Mack hollered. "Put 'em out on the road so we don't have a pileup."

Dallas nodded and retrieved the markers. He walked past Mia who was still trying to get a signal on her phone. Susan appeared to be sleeping, her forehead pressed against the glass. He had thought she was deranged and he still wondered about her sanity, but he could not deny what she said made sense. Dr. Elias was a killer. And he had to be stopped.

Splashing through puddles, he set the cones down a few yards from the back of his truck to signal oncoming drivers. One more set around the turn in the road would be sufficient, he thought, as he slogged onward. Just in time as a dump truck eased to a stop. He got a glimpse of the driver's face, older, scruff of a beard.

But it was the passenger that made his blood run cold.

Archie Gonzales gave him a startled look as he leapt from the cab.

Dallas was at the passenger door before Archie had shoved it fully open. There was no time for Archie to reach for a weapon. Dallas grabbed him by the collar and slammed him against the side of the truck.

"Funny how you always turn up," Dallas snarled.

The truck driver appeared around the front fender. "What's going on?"

"Private business," Dallas grunted. His tone must have convinced the driver.

"I'm going to help clear the road," he mumbled, ambling away over the muck.

Archie tried to move Dallas's hands away, but he did not loosen his grip. "Wasted effort, man. I'm leaving town. My piece of junk rental got stuck in the mud, and I hitched a ride. Going to the airport."

"Leaving? Why?" It occurred to Dallas that he might have been wrong about what had happened at the river. "Did you arrange to have Peter Finnigan killed?"

"Guy who bought it in the river? No. But I have to say, I didn't see that coming. Nice piece of work. Cell phone trigger?"

"Yeah, and I'm sure you've got a cell phone handy."

"Who doesn't? It wasn't me, though. As I said, I'm out of here."

"Explain," Dallas said, applying pressure to Archie's windpipe.

He squirmed. "I was following you and Mia, like I'm paid to do. Don't know who blew up this Peter guy, but I'm thinking it's probably the doctor. He's the one who looped me in. Or maybe his wife."

Mia ran up in time to overhear, cheeks pink, rain rolling down her long hair. "Dr. Elias contacted you in Miami?"

"He contacted Mr. Garza. Tipped him off that you were in Spanish Canyon, and that's why I got sent here." Archie shot her a look. "What did you do to cross that doctor? He's more ruthless than my boss."

"Oh, no," Mia said. "He knew Cora was going to tell me, warn me about what she'd learned. He must have been tracking her emails."

He shrugged. "Don't care. Not my business. I was sent to find the stash."

Mia let out a cry. "But I don't have any money. How many times can I say it? Hector didn't leave me a thing. How can I convince you?"

"Already done. Seems brother Reuben went to see Hector and explained that you and tiny tot were in trouble. Hector came clean. His stash was in Miami all along. Mr. Garza has his money, and my job here is done."

Mia shook her head and let out a sigh.

"Not done," Dallas growled. "You led Gracie up to the roof. She could have been hurt. You have to pay for that."

Archie managed a choked laugh. "Lying to a kid isn't against the law. People do it all the time."

"We'll see if the police agree. You broke into Mia's house, too. Better get a lawyer."

Archie struggled under Dallas's grip. "Don't have time for that. This whole county's gonna be underwater and I want to go home."

"Well," Dallas said, anger at the fear Archie had caused Mia still bubbling in his veins, "this just isn't your day."

Rain stung his face as he turned Archie around. "Mia, there's some rope in the back of the truck."

She dashed through the rain back up the road.

A trickle of mud ran down from the mountainside and past Dallas's feet.

"I hate Colorado," Archie spat.

"Should have stayed in Miami." Dallas could not prevent a feeling of satisfaction from sweeping through him. Maybe the cops wouldn't charge Archie with anything, but upsetting his easy escape was a small triumph. At this point, he'd take what he could get. Archie first, Dr. Elias next.

Another wave of muck flowed under the truck and across the road. Dallas looked through the sheeting rain. The mountainside was black, denuded a few years back, he estimated, by a wildfire.

The ground trembled under his feet.

Archie's eyes rolled as he tried to process what was happening.

There wasn't time.

With a roar the mountainside fell away into a river of mud that swept toward the truck.

He thought he detected a scream, Mia's scream, but it was lost in the rumble of movement as the mud carried Archie, Dallas and the truck over the cliff.

THIRTEEN

The river of black engulfed Dallas and Archie, the cacophony swallowing up Mia's scream as she struggled to keep her footing on the trembling road. For a moment, she thought the entire stretch would be sucked up by the massive flow, like a monstrous inverse volcano. There was nowhere to run.

As the movement of the earth slowed, the mighty roar ebbed to a murmur. The flow softened into a trickle and then, eerie silence. Her heart cried out for Dallas. She half stumbled, half crawled, along the edge of the road, wiping the rain from her face. Down below was a sea of mud, coating the steep slope, blanketing the trees, blotting out everything it touched. The upended truck had caught on a trunk, wheels spinning lazily above the black ooze that imprisoned it.

"Dallas," she screamed.

The truck driver and the man with the chain saw raced up.

"Two men are down there," Mia screamed, trying to discern a path she could take to reach them.

"Make that one," the truck driver said, pointing.

A mud-caked figure detached itself from the mess, struggling upright.

The men tied a rope to a tree at the edge of the road and

lowered it down. The man grabbed it and hoisted himself up, hand over hand.

Was it Dallas or Archie? Mia found she was holding her breath as the victim fought to pull himself up from the pit. When he was within a few feet of the top, the men reached over and grabbed his arms.

With one synchronized heave, he was pulled over the edge. On hands and knees, he crouched, sucking in a breath. Mia pressed close, unable to force out the question.

"Man," Archie said, wiping a layer of mud from his face. "I really hate this state."

Mia's breath choked off as she ran to the edge again. There was no movement from below, no sign of Dallas.

No, Lord. Please, no.

"I'll try the radio," the truck driver said gently. "We'll call for help."

The other man helped Archie to his feet and moved him away from the slide. Mia stared down into the muck. *Think, Mia.* She spotted the place where Archie had emerged, just behind a stand of three trees that had caught the truck. The thick trunks would have deflected some of the force of the earth flow. If Dallas was there…

"Hey, lady," she heard someone call, as she climbed over the roadbed, clinging to the rope as her feet sank in the mud.

What am I doing? What if I drown in this smothering blanket?

What if she did?

What would she have to show for her life? A perfect daughter, yes, and a heart choked with so much anger, hurt and distrust that it was nearly drowned already. *I've wasted time being afraid. I'm sorry. So sorry.* Her soul offered up the words and it was as if they rose up to the clean, storm-washed air above, even as her body sank into the filth below. A sense of calm ate away at the panic. Mud oozed and sloshed around her, her legs sinking in up to her thighs and then her waist until she was more swimming through it than climbing down. When she came level with the truck, she pulled up the rest of the rope and tied it around herself, transferring her grip from the rope to the sturdy truck fender.

"Dallas," she called. The rain drilled tiny craters into the mud surrounding her. Everything was so monochromatic, a sea of black. She would have to edge around the front of the truck to be able to see beyond. Fingers cold and caked with slippery mud, she groped her way along. A metal shard on the fender nicked her palm.

A few more feet to go, sodden soil sucking against her every inch of the journey, she made her way around the fender.

As she'd suspected, beyond the stand of tightly clustered trees was a space relatively unscathed by the flow. He was not there. Body tingling with despair she scanned frantically.

"Dallas," she yelled again.

A small movement caught her eye. She'd been mistaken. Among the roots of one of the massive trees, she saw him, lying on his side, covered with mud, as black as the shadows that cloaked him.

She scrambled along, fitting between the trees, and made it to his side.

Breathing, let him be breathing. With a shaking hand, she brushed some of the cloying mud from his face.

His eyes blinked open, and it seemed at that exact moment, something inside her opened up, too. She leaned her cheek on his forehead. "Oh, Dallas" was all she could manage.

His eyes widened, the whites brilliant against his mud-streaked face. The breath caught in her throat, and she realized she'd never seen such a truly spectacular sight as those black irises, regarding her soberly, flaming to life as his senses returned. She reached out and stroked his face, running her fingertips along his forehead, his cheeks, again and again, until she began to believe he was really and truly alive.

Was it relief she saw in his eyes? She might have thought it joy, but why would it be so? Her brain reminded her what her heart did not want to acknowledge: she was a job, and she had every right to be angry at this deceiver whose hand she now clung to, their filthy fingers twined together. He had tricked her and withheld the truth from her.

Yet it was definitely not anger she felt, nor anything close to it. And that scared her more than the mudslide. She let go.

His lips moved, but she couldn't detect any sound until she leaned close.

"That was a wild ride," he muttered.

She laughed. It was absurd. Nestled in the mud up to her knees with a man who'd nearly been buried under tons of mountain, rain sheeting down on them both, she could not hold in the relieved giggle that bubbled from her mouth.

"I thought you were dead," she said, biting her lip to steady her frayed nerves.

"So did I, for a while there," he said, struggling to pull himself to a sitting position, letting loose a shower of broken twigs and debris.

"Are you hurt?"

"Dunno yet." Clods of dirt fell away as he moved, the rain washing some of the grime from his face. He stared at her, his gaze so intense it made her look away. "I'm just glad you didn't get sucked down here with me."

"No, I got here under my own steam."

Eyeing the slope he shook his head. "Incredible. Why didn't you wait for help?"

She gave him a casual shrug. The truth was, she did not

fully understand why she had done something so rash, for him, when the hurt still echoed inside. "Seemed like the thing to do after only one of you made it out."

He stiffened, as if remembering. "Archie?"

"He climbed up, unharmed, of course."

"Of course." Dallas tried to get to his feet. "We've got to get back up there. Go to the police."

He stood too quickly, staggering backwards. She quickly shoved her shoulder under his. "Slow. I can't carry you out of here, so don't push too hard."

He considered the slope and groaned. "That's a long way back up."

She showed him the rope tied around her waist, ridiculously pleased at the respect on his face.

"Smart thinking to tie the rope."

"I'm not as good at rescue as Juno, but I do my best."

He laughed, winced, and put a hand to his ribs.

"Broken?"

"Probably bruised, but I'll make it."

She unknotted the rope from her body so they could both grab hold. They began the arduous ascent, first climbing around the ruined truck and then struggling up the slope, stopping every few feet to rest, sinking sometimes to their knees, sometimes to their waists in the sticky mud. When he stumbled back, she would grab his arm, holding him steady until he regained his balance. When she slowed, mired down by the cloying mass, he pulled her through the worst of it. Though she did not want his help, she was grateful. Now that the adrenaline from the rescue was depleted, every muscle in her body seemed to resent the effort it took to climb back to the road.

Mack met them halfway down, lowered on another rope fed to him by the truck driver. Mia could have cried in relief when the big man grasped her around the waist and they were hauled to the top by the men, and, to Mia's surprise, Susan.

Susan helped her to sit on the fender of Dallas's truck while Mack went back down the slope to assist Dallas. From somewhere Susan produced a handkerchief and wiped the grit from Mia's face as best she could.

The rain continued to thunder all around them, and now she found herself pleased with the downpour that washed some of the clinging film of mud off her clothes. She felt light and lifted inside, as if she'd somehow left some of her anger at the bottom of the cliff. She was not ready to forgive, not yet, but it did not stop her from enjoying the relief that came from putting down some of her burden. Quietly, she thanked the Lord for blessing her and Dallas with another day of life. How odd to feel thankful. How very strange and foreign.

Dallas was helped over the top, and he walked gingerly over to join her. "Archie's gone," he said morosely. "He got away again."

Mia shook away her strange ponderings, and rubbed at a scrape on her arm. "Good riddance. I never want to see him again. I hope he's right that Mr. Garza is finally satisfied."

"He's got no reason to go after you anymore," Dallas said. "Hector gave him what he wanted."

"Only when he had to."

"Because he heard you were in danger."

She felt shamed. "Yes, I guess so. He loves us, in his own fashion."

"That's one thing he has right." He held her gaze and she found she could not look away. Had the rain become warmer as it fell? The wind melodious as it swept along the road? Had Dallas become even more attractive, filthiness aside? Could be it was all colored by relief, she concluded.

Mack called out from the spot where the tree had fallen.

"I'm going to help clear the road," Dallas said.

"I'll help, too," Mia insisted.

He started to protest and then sighed. "It won't do any good to tell you to wait in the truck, will it?"

"Not one bit," she replied, walking straight to Mack and the truck driver. "Thank you for helping us out of that mess. We're ready to pitch in and clear the road."

Mack chuckled. "And I had you pegged for a city girl."

Mia shot him a sassy smile. "A city girl who's ready to get home to her daughter. Are you going to fire up that chain saw or am I?"

Mack and Dallas exchanged amused looks. In a matter of thirty minutes, Mack sliced off enough of the fallen tree to allow vehicles to squeeze by. Mia, Dallas and the truck driver hauled the branches out of the way while Susan continued to try to get a cell phone signal.

After a shaking of hands all around, Mack and the driver loaded up in his vehicle and the others in Dallas's truck. Mia could not hold back a sigh as she slid onto the passenger seat and Dallas got behind the wheel. The old, cracked vinyl felt like a cloud of comfort compared to the scraping she'd enduring traversing down the cliffside and back up again. It was sheer bliss to be out of the hammering rain. The mud clinging to her skin coated her with an earthy funk.

What she wouldn't give for her favorite lavender lemon bath scrub that Gracie said smelled like candy. She sat up, a current of memory stinging everything inside.

"What?" Dallas said. "Are you hurt?"

"I just thought of something." Mia turned to Susan in the backseat. "You followed Catherine to Peter's house. How long was she there?"

Susan considered. "Only a few minutes. She pounded on the door, but he didn't answer at first. Finally he opened up, they exchanged a few words, and Peter grabbed the photo out of her hand and slammed the door closed. She went around the back and looked through the windows but he refused to let her in. After she left, he came outside and that's when I caught up with him."

"It occurred to me that if Catherine lingered awhile, she also could have put something in Peter's duffel bag while Susan and Peter were inside."

Dallas let out a low whistle. "Is Catherine in on the whole business?"

Mia gave voice to the question that was burning inside her. Peter's duffel bag was already in the boat when they arrived. "Did you see Catherine put anything in Peter's duffel bag?"

"I couldn't see down to the water from where I was in the house," Susan said.

Mia bit back a frustrated sigh.

Was Catherine Elias an unwitting cog in Elias's schemes? Or did she have her own part in Peter Finnigan's death?

Though Dallas had the wipers set at full speed, they hardly kept up with the water sheeting across the glass. His head was pounding a rhythm that matched the throbbing in his ribs. There was no option to drive fast, though he had to fight the urge to ram the gas pedal down. Dr. Elias was a murderer. And his wife, Catherine, might be his partner in crime. Most likely, Elias had taken care of Finnigan, who could prove his guilt. But Mia and Susan could still expose him, and there was the photo tucked under the visor in his truck. The miles passed excruciatingly slowly back to Spanish Canyon.

They headed straight for the police station, against Susan's wishes.

"That detective, Stiving, he won't hear anything bad about the precious Dr. Elias. He's protecting him. Could be the doctor has him on the payroll, even. We can't go to the police here."

"There isn't much choice, Susan," Dallas said. "We'll talk to the chief."

"And you trust him?" she demanded.

"He's given me no reason not to." But Stiving had.

Mia straightened, clutching her phone. "Got a signal. There's a message from Antonia. She got word to evacuate a half hour ago. She packed up Gracie and Juno. They're heading for the airport. She said she'll wait in the parking terminal until we get there." She groaned. "I feel like I should go meet them right now."

"As soon as we report what you…" He broke off as they took the main road into town. The paved surface was covered by inches of water. Shop owners and police officers worked side by side in the rain, filling sandbags. They were fighting a losing battle, as the water was already lapping the sidewalks. Soon it would be spilling through doorways and flooding the businesses all along the block. The police station was obviously evacuating, officers and volunteers carrying boxes and equipment to a waiting van.

Dallas tried to park nearby, but he was waved at by a drenched police volunteer. "Can't stop here. Cantcha' see we're flooding?"

"It's an emergency."

He eyed Dallas and Mia skeptically. "Wet and dirty, but y'all look fine to me. Nobody's getting into the station right now."

Dallas kept his temper with serious effort. "We have to speak to the chief. It's urgent."

"Chief's already gone to our mobile station in Pine Grove. Stiving's out on a call, and every available officer is assisting the fire department. Sorry, can't help you unless you want to drive to Pine Grove and see if they have time for you."

Dallas was about to fire off an angry reply when Mia took his arm. "We'll go to Pine Grove. It's on the way to the airport, anyway."

A pang of grief stabbed at his insides. The airport would be their goodbye, the last time he would ever see her and Gracie. He rolled up the window and drove through the water. Pine Grove and the airport. End of the line. There was no way to stop it. He knew it was better, anyway. Mia and Gracie needed to be safely away from the floods and Dr. Elias. Once they were away, securely settled in Florida, Elias would pay for what he did to Cora, Susan and Finnigan.

Dallas would see to it.

They took the road to Pine Grove, which would provide a higher elevation for the police to regroup. The locals told of floods that had occurred some twenty years before, but nothing like this, and the town was simply not prepared for such a magnitude of disaster.

"Where will you go, Dallas?" Mia said, breaking into his thoughts. "Will you wait until the water recedes and live in the trailers still?"

Why would he? The only thing that meant something was his Search and Rescue classes and he was only filling in for a temporary vacancy. The job would be gone soon, too.

"Dunno. I'll have to ask Juno what he thinks."

Mia smiled and closed her eyes as they drove. She looked very young with her wet hair framing her face, smudged with both dirt and fatigue.

His thoughts wandered. If things had been different and they'd met under other circumstances. Would he have risked a relationship with her? Would she have allowed him past the protective wall she'd built? Might he have stuck around long enough to chip away at it?

Maybe he wouldn't have been brave enough to attempt

it. He would have packed up his unfinished puzzle and his uncomplaining dog and left town rather than face his own vulnerability. He would never know if he would have let the most amazing woman he'd ever known walk out of his life because now it was too late. She was flying away, and it felt like she was taking his heart with her. Despair felt as weighty as the oppressive storm.

He almost didn't have time to slam on the brakes. A car he didn't at first recognize, was stopped in the road, doors open, hazard lights on. Juno stood next to the car.

"It's Antonia," Mia cried, leaping from the truck. He was behind her in a flash. Juno raced up to him, electric with some kind of excitement.

Antonia stood in the rain, body shaking, mouth tight with terror. "Oh, Mia. She's gone. She's gone." Tears rolled down her cheeks as Mia gripped her forearms.

"What happened, Antonia?" Mia demanded, voice hard as glass. "Where's Gracie?"

Antonia tried to answer, but no sound came out. Mia's hands tightened, viselike, around her sister's wrists. "Where is my daughter?"

Sucking in a breath, she tried again. "He took her."

"Who?" Mia's words rang with anguish.

"There was a chair overturned in the road. I got out to remove it. When I turned back, a man was there at the passenger-side door. He...he took Gracie and ran up the road. I heard him get into a car and then he was gone." She heaved in a breath. "Juno barked, but I had him leashed in the back and he couldn't get out. I called the police. They're coming."

"No." Mia's hands flew to her mouth. "No, no. This can't be happening."

"He always wins," Susan said, her own eyes round.

"I'm sorry, I'm so sorry," Antonia kept repeating.

"Who?" Dallas said. "Who was the man? Did you recognize him?"

The look she gave him was pure agony. "I know his face because I looked him up online when you told me he fired Mia." She swallowed. "It was Dr. Elias."

FOURTEEN

Mia saw the ground rush up to meet her as her legs failed. Dallas caught her before she hit the asphalt and carried her back into the passenger seat of his truck. She did not feel him lift her, she could not feel anything except a cold river of terror that seemed out to numb her limbs, her mind, her soul. He had Gracie. Dr. Elias had taken her baby.

"Sit for a minute," Dallas's soothing voice urged.

She felt pressure and realized that Antonia was gripping her hand, squeezing hard enough that her sister's nails bit into the tender skin of her palm. She was speaking, and Mia tried to follow. Antonia told the story in halting bursts. "After I called the police, I checked back with the trailer park. They haven't been ordered to evacuate, yet. It was a hoax."

Dallas said. "He probably pretended to be with the fire department. He told you there was an evacuation order so he knew when you'd be passing by."

Antonia nodded, grief stricken. "He must have been watching, parked around the turn in the road, waiting for us. I should have known. I never should have left her in the car alone. Oh, Mia, what have I done?"

It was as if Mia was watching it all from a distance, like a dramatic play unfolding on the stage in front of her. She should comfort her sister. Decide on the next step.

Find a current picture on her phone to give to the police. Isn't that what the parents of missing children were supposed to do? The faces on milk cartons materialized in her mind. She'd seen the pictures, the sweet little faces printed there, smiling in moments of innocence while the world fractured into a nightmare for the parents who searched desperately for them.

She should take action. Every moment idle meant Gracie was that much farther away.

But she could do nothing but shake, her body vibrating to the rhythm of the shock which her mind could not grasp. The hands in her lap, the hair hanging across her eyes, did not seem to belong to anyone real. Gracie, her heart, the most precious person on the planet, was in the hands of a murdering madman. And Mia was reduced to a mindless zombie.

How could it be real? She was dreaming, in the grip of a nightmare.

The phone in Mia's purse rang. "You should answer it," Dallas prodded gently.

She could not force her fingers into life, so he removed the cell from the outside pocket of her purse and thumbed it awake.

"Hello?"

"I'm glad I thought to get the numbers off your cell phone when you left it in the office. This is Dallas's number, isn't it? The loser? Mia, your choice in men is terrible. Did we learn nothing from the last criminal you became involved with?"

Dallas stiffened. "Elias? Where's Gracie?"

Mia sucked in a breath and forced her teeth to stop chattering. Dallas put the call on speaker phone and the four of them bent their heads together to listen.

"Don't talk to the police," Elias said. "I don't want them involved."

Calm, collected, as if he was orchestrating every terrible moment. "What have you done with Gracie?" Mia tried to shout. Instead it came out as a pathetic whisper.

"She's with me, as you are aware, I'm sure."

"This isn't going to accomplish anything," Dallas snarled. "It's all over. We know the truth about Asa Norton."

He paused. "The truth is relative. I want the photo. I will contact you soon with the location."

"Please," Mia said, her voice breaking. "Don't hurt Gracie."

His tone was slightly offended. "I don't want to hurt her, Mia. I'm a doctor after all." Elias sounded almost as if he was talking to a patient, discussing treatment options or surgical procedures. "This is strictly a matter of self-preservation. Practical. Keep the police out of it, give me the photo, and there won't be any need for me to use violence. She will be returned, in perfect health. I'll call you back soon."

"No," Mia screamed, grabbing for the phone. "I want my daughter. Give me my daughter!"

There was no answer. Dr. Elias had disconnected.

Panic burgeoned through her senses. *Gracie, Gracie, Gracie.*

Dallas was talking, saying something as a police car pulled in behind them.

"Mia." He pressed his mouth to her ear. "Do you want to involve the police? I think we should, but I don't know if we can trust Stiving."

The words circled slowly in her mind. *Police. Stiving.*

The police car ground to a halt on the shoulder. Stiving got out and walked over to them. "What's this all about?"

Antonia looked at Mia. She gave a slow nod. What choice did she have, especially after Antonia already called them?

"It's Gracie. She's been abducted." Antonia shook her head. "Aren't you here about my call?"

His gaze narrowed. "No, I'm here for Mia. Who's been abducted?"

Antonia stared at Mia. She felt Dallas's weighty gaze on her, also. They were asking what she wanted to do. Should she trust that this officer could rescue Mia from Dr. Elias? What was the alternative? She didn't even know where to start looking for her daughter. Panic constricted her lungs until she feared she was going to pass out.

"I'm here to arrest you," Stiving finished.

The words sizzled through her addled senses. Arrest her?

"What?" Dallas barked.

"The tests came back like we thought. Cora's blood-pressure medicine capsules were emptied out and filled with cocaine. It caused her to fall into a coma and stopped her heart. Fire Captain says she wasn't alert enough to snuff out the candle on her bedside table which started the fire."

"I didn't do anything to her medicine," Mia heard herself say. "I just picked it up from the pharmacy. Dr. Elias tampered with it. He must have taken it out of my purse at work while I was in the file room."

Stiving raised his eyebrows. "Pretty crazy scenario. A respected doctor in this town murders an elderly volunteer. With a street drug."

"Cocaine is used in nasal surgery all the time. He had easy access," Susan chimed in.

Stiving shot her a look as if he had not noticed her there until that moment. "And why would he do that, exactly? To gain what?"

"Because he's not the man you think he is," Mia said desperately. "He's a murderer, and Cora was onto him. She—"

Stiving held up a hand. "All right. One thing at a time. You'll have a chance to tell me everything when I get you to jail in Pine Grove."

Dallas slammed a hand on the truck. "Listen. She's telling you the truth. He's got her…"

"Enough," Stiving snapped. "There are only two sets of fingerprints on that poisoned medicine, Mia's and Cora's. If the doctor has access to cocaine at the clinic, then chances are Ms. Sandoval did, too, not to mention the fact that she inherited Cora's property. All of that put together gives me more than enough to arrest her. We're going to jail now and if any of you interferes, you can join Ms. Sandoval."

Stiving was an enemy, Mia knew it then. By the time she convinced him that Gracie had been taken, that Dr. Elias was not the man he seemed, Elias might have killed her. The doctor's words came back to her again.

"You're afraid that you can't trust yourself, your choices, your judgments."

He'd seen right down deep into the core of her, the real essence of her weakness. He was a master manipulator, and he was still in control, still pulling her strings as if she was a helpless marionette.

Mia could not trust herself, nor her ex-husband, or the police officer who stood there with the satisfied half smile on his face. She could not trust in the life she had built for her child, the possessions she'd accumulated, the schooling she was so determined to complete. It was not even a certainty that the town of Spanish Canyon would still be there tomorrow, threatened as it was by the menacing floodwaters set to swallow it whole. There was nothing on this earth that she could count on.

From somewhere deep down in her soul, came snippets that she had heard long ago when she was a child, maybe not any older than Gracie.

Trust in the Lord with all your heart…

Seek His will in all you do...
He will show you which path to take.

Trust God. Could she do something so simple and ultimately so very difficult?

Trust God.

Standing in front of her were two people who had done exactly that.

Dallas let the Lord rescue him from a minefield of sin and come out the other side a changed man. Antonia gave up years of anger and bitterness and the Lord transformed her life and filled it to the brim with love. It was time to trust Him to show Mia the way. There was a reason He had given her life and kept her living and right now, that reason she believed with every tiny atom inside her, was to save Gracie.

Armed with that desperate knowledge, and a faith wild and untamed and new, she closed her eyes and surrendered everything to which she had clung so tightly, pride, independence, fear, anger, hurt. *Lord, I trust You. Help me.*

When she opened her eyes she knew. God was there, right there with her as he had been since the beginning. Even when she'd ignored Him. Even when she'd railed at Him and yes, when she'd hated Him. He would be with her through whatever the next few hours brought.

In a flash, she saw the way. There was one person who knew where Dr. Elias had taken her daughter. Only one.

But Stiving would not let her go there, nor would he follow her leads. He would deliver her to jail before he conducted any search for Gracie. If Mia waited, if she let him take her, she would lose her daughter forever.

Please, Lord.

With cold fingers, she slipped the phone in her pocket and stepped out of the car. "All right, I'll go."

"Mia," Antonia cried out. "There has to be another way."

Mia grabbed her in a tight hug. She saw over Antonia's

shoulder the naked anguish on Dallas's face. "It's all right," she whispered to her sister. "Tell Stiving everything. Convince him, if you can."

"What?" Antonia mumbled through her tears. "Where…"

"I'm sorry," Mia said to Antonia and Dallas. She locked onto his wondrous black eyes.

Something in her tone must have told him what she was going to do. He shook his head, hand raised to stop her. With all her strength, she shoved her sister backward, causing her to stumble into Stiving, who toppled against his car door and they both went down in the mud.

Mia ran as fast as she ever had in her life, heading for the rain-soaked forest, running toward the only way she could think of to save her child.

Dallas was thunderstruck. Juno barked and raced after Mia, thinking perhaps that it was some sort of game, until Dallas called him back. He stared as Mia raced over the uneven ground, making for the crowded wall of trees. She ran, fleet as a deer, disappearing between the branches.

Dallas helped Antonia and Stiving to their feet, shock and disbelief rocketed through him in waves. Had Mia really just run from the police? How could she think such a rash move would help find Gracie?

But would he not have done the same thing to find his brother?

Or Mia? He swallowed. Yes, he would.

Stiving barreled toward the trees, making it only a few yards, stumbling and slipping, before he must have come to the conclusion that he had no hope of catching up with her. He turned back to the car, rage suffusing his cheeks with red.

Antonia stood in shock, hands pressed to her mouth, staring in the direction her sister had just taken.

"Bad move." Stiving was on the radio now, calling for assistance in apprehending Mia Verde Sandoval.

The radio exchange seemed to snap Antonia from her inertia, and she started in on him before he could get back in the car. "Her daughter's been kidnapped by Dr. Elias. Whether you want to believe it or not, that's what happened. Dispatch will confirm it. I called it in moments before you arrived."

Stiving's lip curled. "I will confirm it, after I bring your sister in."

Dallas offered up everything he knew about Peter Finnigan's death. Susan reluctantly confirmed the facts until Stiving held up his hands. Was it Dallas's imagination, or did he see the slightest sign of belief on Stiving's face?

"All right. I've got enough to look into. I'll send anyone available to help search for the girl, but you have to know that Mia made an idiotic choice running from the police."

"She wouldn't have done it, except that Gracie's life is in danger," Antonia fired back.

"Seems to me she used that bit before, when she took the kid and went on the run after she served her jail time."

"She knows that was a mistake. She wanted to keep Mia away from her father," Dallas said through clenched teeth.

Stiving ignored him, took pictures of Antonia's car and checked it thoroughly before he ordered her to move it off the road. "They just radioed me that they're ordering evacuations of Spanish Canyon. This road will be jammed. I have to go back to town. You three should head to Pine Grove and wait for me there."

"My sister…" Antonia began.

"Your sister is now a fugitive, and she'll be treated as such." He climbed in the front seat. "If you help her in any way, you're aiding and abetting. Remember that." Tires squelched across the road as he did a sharp U-turn and headed back toward Spanish Canyon.

Dallas considered for a moment, trying to corral the thoughts stampeding through his brain. Mia would not hesitate to sacrifice her own life to save Gracie. Right or wrong, she felt she had no other choice than to run. He had to intercept her. Urgency burned like acid through his veins. "Take Susan and go to Pine Grove."

"What am I supposed to do there?" Antonia demanded. The angry quirk to her lips was so like her sister he almost smiled.

"Convince them to look for Gracie. Get to the chief if you can." He shot Susan a look. "And don't let this lady out of your sight."

"Where do you think he took Gracie?" Susan asked.

"I'm not certain."

"Promise me you won't hand me over to Thomas, even if you do find him," she said, staring at Dallas with those oddly haunted eyes. "You are not that kind of man, I think."

"You're right, and I'm hoping you're not the kind of woman who would walk out on a mother and child. We'll need your testimony to bring Elias down once and for all."

She looked away. "I don't know what kind of woman I am anymore. Before I was just angry, but now..."

"It's time for you to decide." He faced her full-on. "You've been hurt and lost your husband. Now there's a little girl involved." He heard Antonia gulp back a sob. "She needs her mommy, and you can help put things right, but not if you run away. Do you understand?"

She cocked her head. "Yes, I do."

"Then stay with Antonia. When we find Mia, we'll need you to back up her story." He reached out and squeezed Susan's forearm. "This time, the doctor is going to pay for what he's done, I promise."

She nodded slowly.

He started for the truck.

"But where are you going?" Antonia cried. "How can you help Mia?"

"It's my job to protect her, remember?" He opened the truck door.

"You're not just doing a job," she said quietly. "It's something much more than that."

He allowed a moment to acknowledge that she was right. Mia was not a job, she never had been. Not to him. "Juno and I are going to find her."

A freshening wind pulled at Antonia's wet hair as the rain continued to fall. "Do you know where she's headed?"

"I have a pretty good idea."

She came close and gripped his hands. "You have to find her. And Gracie."

"I will," he said, a sense of resolve turning all his fears and uncertainties into hard steel in his gut.

I will.

FIFTEEN

Dallas pulled the truck off the road, crunching across the tall grass, making his own trail to a rocky outcropping behind which he parked. He picked up Mia's purse and offered a sniff to Juno. It was probably completely unnecessary. He had always thought that Juno understood much more than the average member of his species. Juno already knew that he was going to look for the small, determined woman who had crashed through the heavy carpet of grass. Perhaps he thought it was one of their many training exercises where he would be sent to discover a prearranged "victim."

"Find," he commanded anyway.

Dallas watched him run, graceful loping strides over the uneven ground, tail wagging with sheer joy at the prospect of engaging in a search. Mia was no doubt heading for Dr. Elias's house to talk to Catherine. It would be feasible to go there and wait for her to turn up, but he did not want to leave her plunging through a heavily wooded area, wanted by the police and not in her right mind with worry about Gracie. She could fall, break an ankle, sustain a concussion. He shut down the worrisome scenarios.

Juno returned after a short while, alerted with his ear piercing bark, and then disappeared again, scrambling up a twisting road which might have once been a logging trail. Dallas hiked onward, the muddy ground clinging to his boots, rain dripping from his hair. The trail crested the top of a wooded hill and drifted back down toward the highway.

Every now and again, Juno would return and bark, a sign that he had tracked Mia and perhaps even found her already and why didn't Dallas get a move on it and pick up the pace, already? Dallas smiled. They'd cross-trained together, Juno and his awkward human, and the dog was fully capable of both tracking and trailing, and air scenting, but Juno always seemed to relish the opportunity to be off leash and following his impeccable nose toward a rescue. Other dogs could do the tracking on leash.

It never ceased to amaze him. With his paltry sense of smell, he could detect nothing but the odor of rain-washed ground and pine. Juno was easily able to discern the scent left behind by the 40,000 skin cells dropped each minute by his human quarry. Not only that, he could pick that scent from a world awash in odors. Dallas had worked with or known canines that detected everything from cadavers, to explosives, to smuggled fruits and vegetables. And now, his chance to find one small amazing woman lost in a sea of giant trees, all depended on Juno's amazing nose.

Dallas kept himself in high gear. In spite of the aching in his ribs and the pounding rain, he increased his clip until he was at a near jog, avoiding patches of slippery pine needles and puddles as best as he was able. She could not be that far ahead, but her pace was impressive, considering she too had survived a mudslide not many hours before.

Time ticked away, sucking up the minutes until sundown. It was edging toward six o'clock. One more hour of daylight. Juno could track at night, they'd spent enough hours training at it, but Dallas was not as surefooted in the dark, and neither was Mia. She had to be cold and terrified.

And what about Gracie? Was she frightened? Had he hurt her? Bound her? The thought haunted him.

The way ahead was overgrown, thick underfoot with soggy debris and crowded overhead by tree limbs, weeping icy droplets down on him. And then, without warning, the trail was gone. They found themselves in a forest that showed no signs that it had ever been penetrated by humans for any reason. He listened to the incessant dripping. Wind played with branches and loosed more water down upon them which Juno blasted away with a vigorous body shake.

Juno stopped and nosed around for Mia's scent. With still victims on fair-weather days, the scent rose in a neat cone, emanating from the search target. Today the rain, shifting winds and highly active target, was making the search more difficult. It seemed likely that Mia would stop at some point, perhaps to try and use the GPS on her phone to locate Catherine's house, or simply to rest, to hide.

His heart was pounding and muscles fatigued after the brisk climb. Falling away to his left was a small hollow of firs, clustered close enough together to protect from the rain. She would head there, to regroup.

"Mia," he called. No answer but a quick darting movement from behind the trees. He charged toward it.

Juno stopped him with an impatient bark.

"She's down there," he said as much to himself as the dog, ignoring another louder bark from Juno.

He half ran now, wishing his stiff leg and ribs would work in harmony with the rest of his limbs. He'd spent years, his whole adult life, really, combing through wild corners of the world, quiet forests and ruined buildings, creek beds and mountaintops, searching, searching. Sometimes he and Juno had found the target and he'd celebrated. Sometimes they didn't get there in time and they grieved together. After every mission, the need to search always returned. There would be another someone to find, another search to be taken on, a restlessness that told him he had not yet discovered the person he was destined to find.

"Mia," he shouted again, earning another bark from Juno.

He plunged into the clearing, moving so fast he skidded a good couple of feet before he stopped his forward momentum. The Stellar's Jays in the shrubs shot out with a deafening screech, taking refuge in the branches and squawking their displeasure. The air was heavy with the scent of wet grass and decaying leaves.

He completed a rough circle of the hollow, sinking up to his ankle in water at one point. Mia wasn't there. Bending low, he peered under the taller bushes, searching out any hiding places.

No Mia, nor any sign she had ever been there. Juno stared at him. Recrimination. He'd broken his own rule. Trust the dog. Dallas hadn't.

Early on in his career in search and rescue, a mentor watched him disregard a seemingly impossible positive alert from his dog. That's when Dallas had learned the term "intelligent disobedience."

If you've got a smart dog and you have learned to trust each other, let the dog think for himself. Juno had, and Dallas had disregarded him.

He dropped to a knee in the soggy grass and gave Juno a scratch. "Sorry, boy. I messed up. You're in charge now."

Juno accepted the apology by licking a raindrop off Dallas's chin, before he sprinted back in the other direction. Dallas tried to do the same, stumbling on the uneven earth and slapping aside branches as the slope became steep. He'd lost time with his dumb mistake. He prayed it wasn't too late. As the terrain grew more and more rugged, he had to resort to using his hands to hold on to tree trunks and exposed roots as he hauled himself upward, arriving at the top to find they'd looped back to the road.

Fifty yards ahead a yellow truck was stopped, the passenger door open.

And Mia was just stepping in.

"Mia," he shouted. Juno had almost reached her when she pulled the door closed and the truck rumbled away down the road, leaving Juno and Dallas alone on the rain-soaked highway.

Mia's heart plummeted as she eyed Dallas in the sideview mirror, Juno trotting back over to him as the truck pulled out. He'd come to find her, to help her out of the excruciating mess she'd fallen into. Maybe he'd intended to talk her into going back to the police. Knowing Dallas, he'd more likely determined to help her enact her own desperate plan to find her daughter.

But she could not let him throw his life away on a fugitive. And that's what she was, she reminded herself incredulously.

She realized the woman at the wheel was speaking to her. "Where'd you come from? Popping out of the woods like that, I thought you were Bigfoot, till I realized you're too small and not hairy enough." She laughed, setting her gray curls bouncing. "Name's Fiona. You?"

She smiled, imagining she must look like a deranged hitchhiker. "My name's Mia. I'm trying to get to the Spanish Villa Estates, on the edge of town. Do you know where that is?"

"'Course. Nice digs up there." She eyed Mia more closely, gaze flicking over her jeans and torn windbreaker. "That where you live?"

"No." Mia tried to stick to the truth as much as possible. "My house flooded. I know someone who lives in Spanish Villa. She said she'd help us find a place."

"Us?"

Mia swallowed hard. "My daughter, Gracie. She's four." She could not stop the tears then, hot and fast they rolled down her face. "I'm sorry. We've had a difficult time."

"It's okay, honey," the driver said, patting her hand and offering her a tissue box. "I got three girls myself. All grown now with kids of their own, but I remember how hard it was. Especially when my husband split town." She offered Mia a thermos. "Hot tea. You drink some now."

Mia protested.

"Your teeth are chattering. Drink the tea. I got plenty more."

Mia poured and sipped. The tea delivered warm comfort through her body and it had the added bonus of keeping her busy. Most of all she desperately did not want Fiona to ask her any more questions about Gracie. She could not trust her emotions.

Just get to Catherine and find out where her husband has taken my child.

Fiona kept up a constant commentary about the flooding and the small trucking company that she owned. Mia checked her phone constantly for any message from Dr. Elias. There wasn't any. He was probably enjoying the thought of the agony he'd created.

"Built it myself from the ground up," Fiona was saying. "Got twelve trucks now, out of Pine Grove. That's where I'm headed. Heard they've got the police moved up there during the flooding."

Mia sipped her tea and stared out the window. What else had Fiona heard?

Fiona sighed. "Awww, man. Looks like we got a roadblock."

Mia stared through the water-speckled windshield. Four cars ahead of them were stopped at a set of blockades straddling the road. A police officer, or perhaps a volunteer, swathed in a yellow slicker was making his way down the line, speaking with each of the drivers.

Her hands went icy around the cup. Were they looking for her? Nerves jumping, she darted a glance at the door handle. She could yank it open and jump down. Run away from the road. Right, and broadcast her presence like a signal flare.

The officer finished with the first two cars and made it to the third. It was almost sunset, and he held a flashlight. To search the vehicles for her? The fugitive wanted for murdering Cora Graham?

Fiona shot her a curious glance. "Drink more tea, honey, you're shaking like mad."

She watched the officer straighten and splash along the road, his boots dislodging sprays of water under the rubber soles. As subtly as she could, Mia reached for the door with one hand, fingers gripping the metal catch.

With the other, she kept the cup at her mouth, hoping to help conceal her face.

Her stomach was a lead weight as the cop waited for Fiona to roll down the window.

"Hello, ladies." He peered at Mia. "Where are you headed?"

Don't tell him about Spanish Villa, she begged silently.

"Pine Grove. Shop's up there."

He nodded. "Road's flooded ahead. Going to redirect you east about ten miles and then you can double back."

Fiona sighed. "I should have listened to the weather reports more closely."

"More rain coming. Just evacuating the lower elevations now, but might need to expand that." He looked closer at Mia. "You all right, miss?"

"Yes, I'm okay. I needed a ride, and Fiona was kind enough to stop for me."

"That right?" He took in the bedraggled hair, the

scratches on her face from her plunge through the trees. Was there a dawning of recognition on his face? Would there be a request for an ID next? The roar of her own pulse deafened her.

A slow smile spread over his face. "Great to see people helping each other in times of emergency, isn't it?"

"Yes," she said, her sudden movement spilling some of the tea on her lap. She wiped at it with her sleeve.

"You headed to Pine Grove also?" The officer pinned her to the spot with his hard look. Her breath caught and she could not hide the shaking of her hands.

"I…" Mia started.

Fiona broke in. "I'm taking her to see a friend who's gonna help get her and her little daughter fixed up in a new place." Fiona looked at her watch. "When do you think you'll wave us through? I'd sure like to get this old truck in the barn before nightfall."

The officer gave Mia another long look before he consulted his radio. "All clear," he said and began to wave the drivers on to the detour.

She hardly dared breathe. As they rolled by she kept her gaze fastened out the front window, feeling the officer's eyes on her. How could he not hear the slamming of her heart into her ribs? Guilt had to be written all over her face in vivid ink.

Fiona gave the cop a final wave as she eased the truck by. When they were on the road, a good half mile past the roadblock, Fiona sighed.

"You want to tell me about it?"

Mia started. "No, I just can't. I'm sorry."

"It's all right." Fiona sighed. "I knew whatever it was that happened back there, you were anxious to get away from that guy and his dog."

She'd seen Dallas and Juno. And completely misunderstood. "They weren't…"

Fiona held up a hand. "I don't need to hear about it. You're anxious to get to Spanish Villa and just as eager to avoid the police, but you seem like a nice kid and I've got a soft spot for moms and daughters. Here." Fiona removed a plastic-wrapped sandwich from a bag. "We'll split it."

Mia was going to decline but just then her stomach let out a hollow rumble. Humbly, she accepted the sandwich. "Thank you so much, Fiona. How can I ever repay you?"

"You can tell me I make the best ham-and-pickle sandwich you ever ate."

Mia managed a grin. "I think it might be the only ham-and-pickle sandwich I ever ate."

Fiona laughed. "Close enough. We'll be passing Spanish Villa in about a half hour. Sit back and enjoy these luxurious driving conditions."

And Mia did, eating every scrap of the sandwich and clinging to the knowledge that with every mile, she was that much closer to finding Gracie.

Dallas and Juno endured a miserable hike back to the truck. Dallas kicked himself mentally every rugged step along the way. He'd distrusted Juno and lost his chance to catch Mia. Now he was playing catch-up in a big way.

He called Mia's phone again. No surprise when she did not answer. She didn't want to involve him further. *Involved? Mia I'm more than involved now. I couldn't walk away if I wanted to.*

The thought surprised him. He knew she did not want him in her life, nor Gracie's. And he would never force himself into a situation where he wasn't wanted. All true. But also true was the fact that like it or not, he felt deep down in the place where only truth can survive that he was meant to save Mia Verde Sandoval.

He phoned Antonia. She answered before the first ring had died away.

"Dallas? Did you find out anything?"

The Verde women were strong, determined, practical. It would do no good to sugarcoat, nor would he disrespect her by doing so. In the words of his mother, "Every woman's got a spark, Dallas, and adversity turns it to fire." And oh, how he'd fanned his mother's spark into flame. He'd seen it blazing in her eyes when she'd stumbled upon the gun hidden under the seat of his car. He blinked the memory away.

"I didn't catch up to her." Juno gave him the look. Full confession. "Juno found her but I messed up."

Satisfied, Juno set about licking his paws clean.

"I know where she's going, I'll meet her there. I need Susan to tell me where Catherine lives."

There was muffled conversation as Antonia consulted Susan. "She says it's a street in Spanish Villa." Antonia told him the address.

He set the wipers in motion and started the truck. "Are you both all right?"

"We're at a Red Cross shelter in Pine Grove. The chief is supposedly on his way, says a volunteer." She paused. "I'm hearing radio reports about the flooding. It's really bad— road closures all over and a bridge, the Canyon Creek span, is all but underwater."

Dallas let her talk as he headed off. When she ran down, she said what she most needed to get off her chest.

"I feel helpless. I should be searching since I was the one…"

"Antonia, stop right there. We both know who is at fault here and he's going to pay for that."

She let out a soft breath. "What if you're too late, Dallas?"

"I won't be."

"I'll pray for you."

"That's the best thing I could ask for."

The only thing.

SIXTEEN

Fiona let Mia out on a patch of moonlit road at the entrance to the Spanish Villa housing complex. Mia gripped her hand in thanks. "You've done more for me tonight than you know."

Fiona squeezed back. "Take care of yourself, honey. You're strong. You'll make it through whatever it is that's got you in the crosshairs."

One final squeeze and Mia hopped down, avoiding the mud. The sky was leaden with clouds, but the rain had tapered off to a heavy mist. Though she still felt the grit trapped under her jeans and top, her clothes were more or less dry and her belly was not grumbling, thanks to Fiona's gracious gift of a ham-and-pickle sandwich. Had Dr. Elias given Gracie anything to eat? Fear engulfed her in such a tight clutch she had to stop and fight for breath, steadying her shaking legs by locking her knees. One more check of the phone. Still no message and her battery wouldn't last forever.

Go find out where he's got her, and get your daughter back. She set off.

Enormous houses with red tile roofs and white stucco exteriors perched on well-manicured lots. It was a point in her favor that the houses were spaced far apart and the weather kept residents inside, perhaps packing in case evacuations reached even this higher elevation. She had only been to the doctor's house once, for a clinic party which included all the employees.

Fleeting memories trickled across her recollection of the event. White napkins, delicate cheeses and imported olives, plush carpets and a swimming pool in which Gracie had paddled for hours until her button of a nose was sunburned in spite of the cream. Mia's throat ached with unshed tears until a crazy idea flickered into her consciousness. Was it possible he'd brought Gracie here? Catherine had been at Finnigan's for some reason. If she was just as guilty as her husband, this might be the place they were hiding her.

New resolve flooded her with energy. She practically sprinted to the top of the hill, to the last house at the end of a lonely cul-de-sac. Dr. Elias's house.

Knock on the door? It would give them a chance to lock Gracie away or call the police on her. Heart thundering, she moved closer, trying to piece together some sort of plan. A set of arched windows with fancy iron grillwork decorated the side of the house. Most were dark, but golden light glowed from the farthest one. She moved silently to the edge of the neat stepping-stone walk, keeping to the shadows. Did the doctor have a dog? She didn't think so. Too finicky, too controlling. He wasn't the dog-loving type.

You weren't either, until you met Juno.

And Dallas.

Mia realized that she had changed in a lot of ways since encountering Dallas. She had been too far away to see his face, as she got into the truck and left him on the side of the road, but she could imagine the anger and frustration. It stabbed at her. Why were her feelings a jumbled spaghetti mess whenever she thought of him?

Jaw clenched, she pushed the hair out of her face and

shored up her strength. *He shouldn't have followed me. His job is done.* It was all on her now.

Her and God.

She drew level with the window now, fingers on the cold metal grillwork. A quick look. She readied herself to move when a hand went around her mouth, muffling whatever scream she might have managed.

She thrashed against the strong arms holding her, iron bands that kept her fastened against a rock-hard chest.

"Quiet" came the hissed whisper in her ear.

Dallas held her there for a moment, captive against him, and then slowly he turned her around, uncovered her mouth and pulled her into the shadows behind a potted shrub.

She couldn't decipher her own rattling emotions. He looked down at her, moisture beading on his tousled hair, a scratch running the length of his cheek, hands on hips, lips hard with anger. "Mia…" he began, then with a sudden rush he pulled her close and kissed her, palms cradling her head.

The warmth rushed through her in a delicious wave and she kissed him back, forgetting for a moment, everything but the elation that swept through her. A tide of warmth, safety and belonging thundered through her, beating back the desperate fear. When they both ran out of breath, he pulled away and put his forehead to hers.

"Sorry. Shouldn't have done that. You're a pain in the neck to keep track of."

She laughed, a quiet, wobbly chuckle that emerged over the sparks still showering through her. "Where's Juno?"

"He's in the truck because he's not good at quiet. And he's massively upset about it. What did you see inside?"

"I didn't get that far."

He started toward the window.

She grabbed his wrist. "Dallas, I've thrown everything

away to find my daughter. You shouldn't. You have a future without us. I don't want you going to jail for me."

The moonlight flecked his eyes with an inner glow. "Noted." He continued to the window and looked inside.

"Didn't you hear me?"

"Yes," he said, still peering into the house. "I heard you, but I'm not obeying. There's a difference."

She huffed, uncertain whether to be angry or pleased.

He moved away from the window. "Catherine's in the back of the house. It looks like there's a living room that opens onto the patio. Let's see if we can get in that way."

"What if Dr. Elias is inside?"

"Unlikely. His car isn't in the garage."

Mia sagged. "I was hoping that he brought Gracie here."

"Don't think so, but we'll find out where. Let's go."

"Dallas," she tried again to stop him. This time she put her palms on his chest, feeling the strong beating of his heart. How could she tell him what it meant that he had come to find her? And that she could not allow him to stay? "This is wrong, breaking into someone's house. If you help me do this, there's no going back."

"No, Mia," he said slowly. "This is right, that I'm here with you now and we're going to get your daughter back."

"It's not worth it for you. I can't repay you in money, or…" She looked at the ground.

He tipped her chin up, his thumb gently tracing the curve of her lower lip. "I know you have a life to build somewhere else. I understand that. This isn't about payment. It's about what's right."

She closed her eyes tight. "Everything's mixed up, Dallas. How can you be sure what's right?"

He waited until she opened her eyes. "You pray and you take your best shot at it."

"I haven't had a good track record figuring out what's right, but…" She faltered. "I've asked His help this time."

Dallas smiled, moonlight illuminating the joy on his face. "Amen to that." He opened his mouth to continue, but instead he pulled her into the shadows. "Security vehicle," he breathed in her ear. "Stay still."

Easy for him to say, she thought, from the circle of his arms. Pressed against his ribs, her chin next to his, her heart was puttering like a motorboat. She was sure it might give out altogether as it ricocheted between comfort at being near him and utter terror about what could be happening to Gracie, to an odd peace that came when she'd given the situation over to God. A mixed up spaghetti jumble to be sure.

When the car passed, she disentangled herself from Dallas and got to her feet, breathing still hitched and unsteady.

"Ready?" he said, infuriatingly handsome in spite of his sodden condition.

"Are you really sure?"

"Mia," he said, cutting her off. "If you ask me that again, you're going to go wait in the car with Juno."

She was not completely sure if he was joking or not, as he headed off toward the patio.

You kissed her? Again? What part of the plan was that, you dope? The woman was running from the law and terrified for her daughter. He had no business kissing her. He willed his gut to stop quivering like jelly at the residual sensation of her lips pressed to his. He felt like Juno when they first worked together and the dog was more interested in rocketing off after enticing birds than engaging in a search and rescue. Impulse had overridden his good sense. Yet he could not deny the irrational happiness that sprang up in his soul that Mia had invited God in.

Still, had he really kissed her? He had. The electricity still tingled through him.

Focus already, would you?

He pulled his mind back to the present. As soon as Catherine caught sight of them, she would call the police or bolt. Since there was no way he wanted to hurt her, that gave them only a few minutes tops to see if they could convince her to rat out her husband or, if she was an accomplice, to bluff her into thinking she and the good doctor were caught.

Not much of a plan, but he couldn't think of anything better.

They reached the patio just as Catherine Elias stepped out. Dallas and Mia watched from behind a screen of bushes as she turned on the propane gas, and a fire pit sprang to life. She watched it burn in silence. The flames danced high in the darkness.

Mia burst out into the circle of light. "Where's my daughter?"

Catherine screamed, hands pressing a file folder to her chest. "What are you doing here?"

Dallas stepped forward so she could see him, too. "Your husband kidnapped Mia's daughter, Gracie. We're here to find out where he took her. Mia said you have a cabin in the mountains. We need to know where."

Catherine's mouth opened in an *O* of surprise. Or was it anger? He couldn't tell. She took a step toward the house, but one step only, eyes shifting in thought.

"Why would he take her?"

She knew something. Maybe everything. "He wants us to hand over the photo that you took to Peter Finnigan that can incriminate him in Asa Norton's murder."

"Asa Norton? The man who drowned all those years ago?" She cocked her head as if listening to the sound of far off music. "Susan's husband."

"Are you helping him?" Mia fired off.

"Helping? You think I helped my husband kill Asa?"

"No, but he also murdered Cora Graham and Peter Finnigan. You might have pitched in for those."

Catherine's mouth went slack. "This is insane. I'm not a murderer."

Dallas could not be sure it was disbelief or lying. Women confounded him. He had no chance of reading her right, but he pressed on anyway. "You went to see Peter Finnigan, just before he was blown up."

"Blown up? What are you talking about? He was perfectly fine when I left him." She sank down on the brick patio wall, heedless of the moisture. "This can't be true."

"It is true," Mia protested. "You know I'm not lying, don't you?"

She chewed on a thumbnail. "I suspected something was going on when that woman Susan showed up, stalking me. He said he'd treated her for a minor injury after her husband drowned and she became fixated with him."

"But you didn't believe him?" Mia pressed.

"Not really. There have been other women," she said wearily. "I suspected Susan was another one of Thomas's flings and he was trying to cover up. But then things started to happen. Cora died. This thug from Miami showed up. And I found Thomas shredding files. These files taken from the clinic." She waved the folder at them. "There's nothing in them now. They're Cora's. Most were destroyed, but I saved one without him knowing. The photo was in it along with a newspaper clipping about Norton's death."

The pieces were beginning to fall into place, Dallas thought. "You recognized your husband in the picture."

"Yes, that's why I went to see Peter Finnigan. I read the paper's account of how Finnigan supposedly tried to save Susan's husband that day. I can't prove it, but I think Thomas was giving Finnigan money, paying him to stay quiet. I found an envelope of cash one time, addressed to

P. Finnigan at his Mountain Grove address. Thomas explained it away, but I always wondered about it."

"Did Peter tell you anything?" Mia asked.

"Nothing. As a matter of fact, he snatched the photo and tossed me out, but I didn't do anything to harm him. And now you say he's dead? Are you sure?"

Dallas nodded. He would never lose the memory of how Finnigan lost his life.

"Why kill Peter?" Catherine mused.

"Both were involved in Asa's death," Dallas said. "Peter must have threatened to tell, so Elias killed him."

"After all these years? Why?"

Mia hugged herself. "Something went wrong."

"Susan's no innocent in all this, you realize," Catherine spat. "She kept quiet about Thomas's involvement all these years instead of going to the police, not to mention the fact that she got millions when Asa died."

"But she can bring Dr. Elias down now." Mia shivered. "So he'll need to kill her, too."

"I didn't want to see it." Catherine looked up at the cloud-washed sky. "I mean, I knew about the other women. I'm not so blind that I couldn't figure that out. I didn't want to believe there was anything else."

"Why didn't you go to the police?" Dallas said. "If you're an innocent in all this?"

She turned haggard eyes on him. "I'm leaving him as soon as I can get my things together. He's a manipulator and covering up whatever he did in the past, but the man is the father of my children. Whatever Thomas has done, they don't deserve to live with his sin. Can you understand that?"

Mia clutched Catherine's hands. "Yes, so you can understand why I need to find my daughter. Please, Catherine, you've got to tell me if you know where he might have gone."

"I don't," she said, detaching herself.

"Where's your cabin?" Dallas watched her mouth tighten.

"He wouldn't abduct a child. He's a lot of things, but he has his own children. He wouldn't hurt Gracie."

"But he did," Mia said. "Your husband called me and told me he had my daughter. You have to face it, just like I had to face the truth about Gracie's father."

"This can't be possible. I would have known I was married to a murderer." Catherine looked away. "What kind of woman wouldn't know?"

"A woman like me," Mia said. "I misjudged my husband, too, Catherine. You feel stupid, vulnerable. And then—" she shot a look at Dallas "—you forgive yourself and you move on."

"I loved him." A tear rolled down Catherine's cheek. "I really did. Maybe I still do."

Mia knelt next to her and took her hand. "Believe me I understand, but your husband has killed and killed again, and now he has my baby." Her voice broke on the last word. Dallas put a hand on her shoulder, trying to squeeze some comfort into her.

"But Thomas is a father himself," Catherine said. "How could he?"

"I think you know deep down that we're right," Dallas said. "That's why you were getting ready to burn this file, isn't it?"

"All the others are shredded. This one only has the clipping left. I…I figured whatever he's been up to, the less evidence the better for my kids."

Mia did not release Catherine's hand. "Even if you can't accept it, would you throw away Gracie's life? A mother couldn't do that to another woman's child."

Her face crumpled. "I'm not a bad person. Really, I'm not."

Dallas sensed they were near to breaking through her defenses. "Then tell her."

Tears cascaded down Catherine's face. "The cabin's near the reservoir, on Sentinel Hill Road."

"Thank you." Mia clutched Catherine in a desperate hug.

"Here," Catherine said, shoving the file folder at Dallas. "Take it. Maybe it will help you prove he's guilty."

Betrayal shone like an exposed wound deep in her eyes.

"I'm sorry," he said.

She waved him away. "I won't be here when you come back. If what you say is true, I'll never come back."

Mia and Dallas left her staring at the fire pit.

SEVENTEEN

Mia was panting hard by the time they made it to Dallas's truck, having had to stop twice to avoid detection by the security people. She still had twigs tangled in her hair from their leafy hiding spots and a new catalogue of scratches. Once Juno was finally convinced to move to the backseat, he could not stop pressing his wet nose to her neck, snuffling her hair until she batted him away.

"Stop, Juno. That tickles."

He responded in doggie fashion by licking her along the hairline which made her laugh.

"I think you blew his mind showing up like this when he was all set to locate you out in the woods."

"Sorry," she said, giving Juno a rub under the chin. "You'll just have to find me some other time." When she'd gotten Juno down to an occasional slurp from the backseat, she called Antonia and put her on speaker phone.

Her big sister alternated between giving her a tongue lashing and expressing heartfelt relief that Mia was now in the company of Dallas and Juno. "I'm still waiting for the chief. Susan's gone to see if she can find a room somewhere for us, but the town is full of evacuees." She huffed. "It's driving me crazy. Every minute I'm thinking about you and Gracie and I want to be doing something to help."

Mia heard her sister start to sniffle. "Don't cry, sis, or

I'll start, too. We're going to get her, Antonia, we got some info from Catherine," she explained, giving her sister the location of the doctor's cabin. Saying it aloud spread an eagerness inside that she felt would burst out.

"You can't go. This is too dangerous," Antonia said.

"What choice is there? He's got Gracie, and I'm a fugitive."

"We have to tell the police where you're heading," Antonia insisted.

Mia's head spun. "No, I won't risk it. I can't."

She looked to Dallas.

"You know where we're going, Antonia." He checked the time on the truck's dashboard. "Give us a two-hour head start, then tell them everything."

If we're not back…if we're too late. Suddenly she could not get enough oxygen. There was no outcome possible except that they would find Gracie, unharmed and get her away from Elias. Forcing a breath in, she grated out the words. "Tell whoever will listen, but you and Susan need to stay there where it's safe." She paused.

"Okay," Antonia said.

"I don't know if Susan is trustworthy," Mia said quietly. "She's unstable, and she benefitted from her husband's death financially."

Antonia lowered her voice. "If she was involved in the murder, why would she come back and blame it on Elias?"

"It makes no sense to me, but I wanted to warn you. I can't stand anything happening to you." She scrubbed at a spot of grit on the knee of her jeans. "I wish I could do this by myself and not endanger any more people."

"You've got help now, Mia. You're not alone. Dallas is there, and Reuben's flying here as we speak. He's devastated about Cora and…and Gracie."

Deep breaths. "I'm going to get her back, Antonia." Mia clutched the phone. "I am going to get my daughter back."

"Be careful, sister."

"I'm used to dealing with criminals remember? I used to be married to one." The joke fell flat. She was about to hang up.

"And I wanted to say—" Antonia rushed on "—I'm sorry I didn't tell you about Dallas. Reuben and I…"

"Were trying to protect me." She sighed. "And so was Dallas. I understand." And she did. Though Dallas did not look at her, she knew from his kiss, from his willingness to risk everything, that he was with her because he cared for her. With a stab of anguish, she also knew there could be no future for them. When she found Gracie, she would move back to Florida and be the best possible parent to her child. She would play it safe and humbly accept any help from her sister and brother-in-law. No more striking out on her own. No more independence at all costs.

And Dallas? He would continue to bounce around the country finding the missing, and living the kind of unfettered freedom that was exactly what Mia and Gracie did not need. He found lost souls and returned them home. She would always picture him that way, even when they had separated for the last time.

A branch snapped loose from the trees and cracked into the windshield, shocking her out of her reverie. Find Gracie. That was all that mattered.

"Be careful," Antonia said. "Please, Mia."

She said she would and disconnected.

Dallas kept the truck at a slow speed which maddened her, windshield wipers slapping out their own relaxed rhythm. "Can't we speed up a little?"

"Roads are dangerous right now, and we don't need any cops or security people taking notice of us."

She huffed. "Why do you have to be so…logical?"

He offered a smile which died quickly away.

"What's bothering you? Aside from the insanity which you've gotten yourself into?"

"Finnigan."

"What about him?"

"The way he died. We know Elias killed Asa Norton and Cora. He used drugs in both cases. Neat. No blood. Almost a peaceful way to die. But Finnigan…"

She saw the explosion in her mind's eye, the bright flower of flame that blew away Finnigan's life before the river took his body. "A bomb seems out of place for Dr. Elias?"

"Maybe I'm wrong."

"Could Catherine be lying about everything? Is it possible she killed Peter for some reason and she's trying to hide it by shifting blame to her husband?" The rest remained unspoken. *Could we be driving into a trap right now?*

"That's part of what's bothering me. I don't know if Catherine or Susan can be trusted."

"The only thing I can be certain of is Susan didn't take Gracie and neither did Catherine," Mia said firmly. "And that's all I care about right now, getting my daughter back."

They ran into two detours which cost them time. It was nearing ten o'clock when Dallas finally started the ascent up Sentinel Hill. Posted signs warned of flooded roads ahead.

The more Dallas slowed, the more frenzy whipped inside Mia. At the top of a winding road, he pulled to the side. "Hang on. Gonna climb up those rocks and check things."

He got out, Juno following. Clouds rolled over the moon, leaving only unreliable patches of light that played across the pile of rocks, marbled with shadows and moisture. Juno sat at the bottom, eyes riveted on Dallas's progress as he climbed.

He'd just scrambled to the top when Mia's phone rang. Dr. Elias.

She scrambled to press the button. "Hello?"

"My apologies for making you wait so long, but we developed car trouble on the way."

She fought for calm. "Where?"

"We're at the cabin, top of Sentinel Hill. Roads are flooded so you'll have to be creative. Bring the photo. If you aren't here by midnight, there will be consequences."

Consequences. Mia's nerves turned to trails of ice. "I want to talk to my daughter right now."

There was a sound of movement.

"Mommy?"

"Gracie." Tears rained down Mia's face, her heart rose up and twined itself with those two precious syllables. "Are you okay? Did he hurt you? Mommy's coming."

Dallas climbed down and joined her. With icy fingers, she held the phone between them.

"We're going on a boat 'cuz…"

The phone was yanked away. "Gracie!" Mia screamed.

"Midnight." The phone clicked off. Mia stared. "She sounds okay, like he hasn't hurt her. Yet."

Dallas pressed her shoulders. "She's all right. Hang on to that. Gracie is all right."

Inside she repeated the mantra. Gracie was all right.

Until midnight.

Dallas wanted to reach through the phone line and pummel the man. Mia did not resist when he urged her back into the truck. She clutched the cell as if it was somehow still connecting her with Gracie.

"He's desperate for the photo. He won't do anything to her until we deliver it."

She nodded mechanically, like an automaton. He wondered if she would withstand his next bit of news.

"This area is bisected by a river that feeds into a lake. It's all flooded. There's no way I can drive any farther."

Some flicker of life in her eyes. "Where is the cabin?"

"On the other side of that ridge. The place is flooded, and he can't drive out, either. He's going to try to boat out of here. He's probably booked a flight and has his escape all lined up."

Her eyes were dull, breath coming in harsh gasps. "Mia, are you listening?" Was she going into shock? "We need to hike in and probably swim, there's no other option. Let me go ahead, with Juno. You don't have to…"

She fired back to life, fixing him with a look more ferocious than some of the gang members he'd tangled with. "I'm going." He was smart enough to know any arguing the point would get him nowhere but left behind. Juno had no complaints either, even though the sky was delivering more rain. The dog would prefer monsoons to the backseat of a truck any day of the week. He didn't want Juno in danger any more than he wanted Mia to be, but there was nothing to be done about that either. He threw up a prayer and let out a sigh. "Text Antonia. Tell her to fill the cops in on the doctor's call. Okay?"

Her fingers flew across the keys. "All right, let's go."

He removed a pack from under his seat and shouldered it, handing her a bottle of water. "Drink."

"I'm not thirsty."

"Humor me and drink anyway." He poured some into his cupped palm for Juno, who lapped it up, tail wagging and ready to begin the adventure, and drained a bottle himself. He wouldn't suggest they eat the snacks he'd stowed in the pack, though his stomach was empty. He had a feeling it was going to be all he could do to keep up with her. From a supply in his stash, he handed her a plastic bag for her phone and two more for the photo which she double-bagged and stowed in his pack.

Juno gave an excited whine.

"It's okay, buddy," Dallas said. "This time we already know where to find her."

The question was, how would they handle it when they did? There was no more time to think about it as they started across the sodden grass toward the top of Sentinel Hill.

The ground had been transformed to a marsh by the relentless rains. Mud sucked at their feet and shins and each step was a struggle, though Juno seemed to have no trouble with it. There was just enough moonlight peering between the clouds to sufficiently light their way. Some half an hour later they made it to the ridge, flopped down on their bellies and scoped out the cabin.

It was what surrounded the neat, wood-sided structure that concerned him most. The lake, which was normally a stone's throw from the cabin, was now engulfing it, clear up to the doorstep. A boat rolled on the rain-speckled surface, tied to the porch support.

Dallas whistled low. "This place will be under water in a matter of hours."

Worse yet, the cabin was on the far shore, a good quarter mile across the lake. He didn't hazard a guess about the depth. Didn't matter. They had no boat and no car. Swimming was the only option.

She read the question in his mind. "I'm a good swimmer."

"A Miami girl? I'd be surprised if you weren't." He emptied the remaining water bottles out of his pack, keeping only the first-aid kit and foil-wrapped food.

She offered the sliver of a smile. "You travel prepared."

"Sometimes it takes a few days to complete a rescue. Conditions are bad more often than not." He felt her watching. "What?"

"I was so mad about how you ended up in my life and

just now, I was wondering if God put you here in spite of me, to rescue Gracie."

He reached out a finger and traced the perfect line of her cheek and chin. "Maybe He meant for us to rescue her together."

Moonlight captured the tears gathered in her eyes, jewels that she would not let fall. It made them more precious, somehow, the strength that kept them captive there. Mia was a woman of breathtaking courage, who could not see the best things about herself. If she could see what he saw, only for a moment, it would take her breath away.

"You are an amazing woman, Mia Verde."

She blinked, then blessed him with a smile that would live inside his heart with all the most precious memories he possessed. "Coming from you, I take that as a fine compliment. Thank you, Mr. Dallas Black."

What he wouldn't give to kiss her right then, with the rain covering them in glistening droplets and the moon gilding her hair with a million sparkles. He swallowed hard. "When we get across, try for the east side of the cabin where there's only one window. Okay?"

She nodded, stripped off her jacket and without another word waded into the lake. Juno, who had been busy sniffing, gave him a comical double take.

"Yeah, I know it's a strange time for a swim, but you're up for it aren't you?"

Juno, every bit as silent as Mia, ambled right into the water after her.

EIGHTEEN

Cold. It shivered through her body as she swam into the dark water. Juno paddled ahead, turning once in a while to be sure she was still following along. Dallas kept level at her side. She suspected he could easily outpace her, but he, like Juno, was keeping tabs, ever her faithful guardian.

Her muscles fell into a desperate rhythm. Each stroke, every kick and breath brought her that much closer to Gracie. She would force herself to cross this endless watery barrier between herself and her daughter. Despite her effort, goose bumps prickled her skin. Clearing the water from her eyes, she realized she was still no more than halfway across the expanse. Arms tired, legs leaden and she stopped, treading water.

Dallas was next to her in an instant. "Need a rest?"

She was too winded to respond.

He offered his back. "Hold on. I'll tow you for a while."

Sucking in a breath she shook her head, not wanting to add weight to a man she had already burdened so heavily. "I'm okay." She plunged ahead. More minutes, inching along, the void fighting against her in a strange nocturnal race. There was just the frigid water and her weakened body, battling for each and every stroke. Her heart traveled on ahead, calling Gracie's name into the night.

She remembered Hector and Gracie splashing in the warm Miami waters.

"Blow bubbles, *bebé,* like a little fishy." He'd held Gracie against the foaming sea and laughed at the baby kicks and clumsy wiggles she'd tried. "She's going to be a great swimmer," Hector announced, his face shining with love.

Gracie's soft voice echoed through her memory. *My daddy's a bad man.*

Hector was a man who had done very bad things, but also a man who loved Gracie Louise quite possibly as much as she did. It was a fact she had forgotten, or perhaps, she had not wanted to accept. Maybe someday the Lord could make Hector's path straight, too.

And hers. If she could just get to Gracie. There were so many things she had to tell her, to love her through, comfort her against and lift her over. So many waves to be traversed. *Lord, help me, help me.*

Water broke over her face and she sucked in a mouthful. What if Dr. Elias had hurt her? Or worse? Fatigue and fear started to paralyze her limbs. Her teeth chattered. Wind-driven waves splashed again, sending her into a coughing fit.

His arms twined around her, lifting her head out of the water. "I'll hold you. Rest a minute."

She tried to protest.

"We're in this rescue together, remember?"

"Old habits…"

He kissed the tip of her nose and for a moment, she thought he might press his lips to hers. Expectation rippled through her body, but then he turned and she clung to his wide shoulders, feeling the muscles moving along his back. Cheek resting against him, she watched the moonlight catch on the surface dappled by the pattering rain. Almost there. What would they find? She pressed her face harder into his back, strong and soothing, a partner in the lowest moment of her life.

Oh Lord, I don't deserve this man who's risking everything to help me. I have been hard-hearted to him and to Hector. Hector was a criminal, yes, and maybe he always would be, but at that moment with the water lapping against them, she prayed he would be redeemed. He was a sinner who could be good with God's help. Just like a small woman in a very big lake whom she now understood was just as much in need of a savior.

"Almost there," Dallas murmured, calling Juno closer as they neared the other side.

"And Lord, thank you for Dallas," she whispered, completing the prayer and giving it to God.

The wall of the cabin facing them had no windows, except a small one cloaked by heavy curtains. They climbed up on what used to be a wraparound porch which was now covered by six inches of water. Juno levered himself out of the water next to them, immediately shaking his sodden coat with such violence both Dallas and Mia threw up their arms for cover.

Dallas peered around the corner, Mia crowding next to him to see.

A motorboat was tied to the porch rail, and a faint band of soft golden light shone from under the drapes in one of the front windows.

"There's a bag and supplies loaded into the boat," he whispered in her ear. "He's ready to get out of here."

The front door was thrown open. Instinctively, Dallas moved Mia behind him.

"Don't be shy," Dr. Elias called. "Come on in."

Mia pictured Gracie inside. What had the monster done to her? She pushed forward but Dallas stopped her.

"If we don't leave with Gracie in a matter of minutes,

the police are coming in," Dallas shouted back. "It's all over for you."

"Nice bluff," Elias said. "But it's not going to fly. I've been tracking you with binoculars since you started your swim. Now get in here before I lose my patience."

Mia's heart sank. It was a trap, and there was no choice. What had they expected anyway? To surprise the doctor? Snatch Gracie from under his nose? They splashed along the porch until they reached the door.

Dr. Elias held a small lantern in one hand which added a pool of meager light. He wore jeans and a flannel shirt. His face was marred with stubble and darkened by shadows that added years. He looked nothing like the self-assured doctor, a man respected by the townspeople. He looked, in fact, like a man on the edge of desperation.

He pulled the gun from his pocket. "Inside. Now."

Mia went first, Dallas and Juno following.

It was a small cabin, three rooms, a ratty sofa and an old rocking chair, the only furniture. A fire in the small stone fireplace gave off sooty smoke that burned her throat. "Where's Gracie?" Mia demanded.

"In a minute." Dr. Elias gestured to Dallas. "Put down the pack."

Dallas did so.

"You'd better have the photo I requested."

Mia hurried over, wrenched open the pack and thrust the plastic bag containing the picture. "There. I brought what you asked for, now give me my daughter."

Elias took the bag, flicking a glance inside, while keeping the gun leveled in their direction. "Ancient picture. Old lady was thorough. I wonder where in the world she unearthed it." He tossed it into the flames. "The trouble is, of course, other people could follow the same trail Cora did. Maybe you even made copies before you came."

"We didn't," Dallas said. He wondered if Catherine had,

for an extra bit of insurance in case Elias resurfaced in her life someday.

Elias sighed. "In this age of technology, you can't really obliterate anything can you? It's best if I disappear." He shook his head. "Such a waste. I created a good life here, a thriving practice. Raised my kids in Spanish Canyon. I hate to leave it, and them."

"Don't you dare talk to me about your children, after what you did to my child. I want my daughter," Mia shouted. "Where is she?"

Elias laughed. "I have always admired your spunk, Mia Verde Sandoval."

Mia started at a run toward the closed bedroom door which opened abruptly.

"She's here with me," Susan said, stepping over the threshold, holding Gracie's hand.

Mia screamed and ran to Gracie, snatching her from Susan's grasp and sweeping her into a smothering embrace. "Oh, Gracie, my sweet Gracie." Mia cried so hard the tears spilled over onto Gracie's cheeks as Mia planted kiss after kiss on her baby's face.

Gracie looked bewildered, but not physically injured. She wrapped her small arms around her mother and smiled. Dallas's heart tore a bit to see that innocent smile.

"Mommy, you're squishing me," she said. Juno poked a friendly nose at Gracie's leg. "Hiya, Juno."

Mia looked her over. "Are you hurt? Did he hurt you in any way?"

She shook her head. "No, but I want to go home. I don't like it here."

Dallas heaved a sigh. Gracie was safe and his spirit spiraled at the joy of it, but he could not ignore the dread that rose in his stomach as the cost of his error came to light. Somewhere inside, Dallas had known the truth about

Susan. Why had he not thought it out before? "You rendez-voused with the doctor when you gave Antonia the slip by pretending to look for a room, I take it."

She nodded. "Easy."

"And you and Dr. Elias killed your husband together, didn't you?"

"That's so heartwarming, like something you'd see on the big screen." Susan was smiling, watching Mia and Gracie as if she was an adoring aunt, not a murderer. "Yes, we plotted to kill Asa together and afterward, I made the biggest mistake of my life. I bolted."

"Leaving me holding the bag," Elias snapped.

"I was young, and I didn't know what I wanted. I apologized for that, Thomas, over and over," Susan said. "I panicked. But I never stopped loving you, not for one moment in all those years."

So it was some twisted form of love that brought her back to Spanish Canyon. The loathing in the doctor's eyes revealed it was purely one-sided. Whatever fondness Dr. Elias had felt for Susan once upon a time, had evaporated when she collected the insurance money and ran.

Elias's nostrils flared. "You should have stopped loving me. You should have gone on and lived your own life and left me to mine. That's what I told you when you came back but you would not listen."

"I couldn't do that. Our love is too deep." A strange guttural noise came from her throat. "Only I came back to find you had married someone else." Her eyes went hard and flat.

"Catherine is a good woman."

"She's a snoop. If she hadn't taken the photo out of Cora's file, things would have been much simpler." Susan considered a moment. "Well, we're all entitled to a mistake now and then."

Elias groaned. "If you'd stayed away, everyone would

be better off. You got Cora's suspicions up and filled her head with stories that police were corrupt until she decided to confide in these two."

"And Peter?" Dallas asked. He darted a glance around the dismal room, trying to figure out how to keep Gracie and Mia out of the line of fire. "Did he get scared and threaten to tell?"

"He wouldn't have," Elias said, white-knuckling the gun. "Peter would not have said anything no matter how much these two pried, but you arranged for him to die anyway, didn't you?"

Susan gave him a wide smile, sidling around and putting her hand on his cheek. He flinched away. "It was prudent. When Dallas and Mia are gone, we'll have a clean slate. Peter might have decided to spill the beans someday. That's why we arranged this little kidnapping, remember? To clean up the loose ends, as they say in the TV shows." She laughed.

Dallas bit back a groan. She was the one who had, no doubt, alerted Elias when they'd retrieved the picture from Finnigan's, and who'd called the trailer park to arrange the kidnapping. There had certainly been plenty of time for her to do so while Dallas and Mia dealt with the mudslide.

Water crested the threshold, sending the first gush over the floor. Dallas looked for something he could use as a weapon. He saw nothing within easy reach.

"Floodwater's rising," Elias said. The waves quenched the flames in the fireplace with an angry hiss. "Reservoir's full, and it's dumping into the lake."

Susan's eyes were dreamy, her face soft. "We can go anywhere in the world, Thomas. I've still got plenty of money and we can live the life we were meant to. Finally, after all these years. That's what you want, too, isn't it?"

"Too late to ask me what I want." Elias pointed to a narrow ladder in the corner. "Get up in the attic, Mia. Gracie and your hoodlum friend, too."

"You can't," Mia started.

"The guy with the gun makes the rules," Dr. Elias said, "so that means I can. You get up in that attic and take your chances with the floodwaters, or I can shoot you."

It would not be much of a chance, Dallas knew. Locked in the attic, they would drown. No question about it. Antonia would tell the police what she knew, but by then Elias would be gone. "You're a doctor," Dallas said, edging closer and stepping in front of Mia. "You took an oath to save lives. Didn't that mean anything to you?"

A flicker of emotion rippled across his face. "I was a good doctor. I helped a lot of people, and they loved me in this town. I just made a mistake a long time ago."

Susan stepped back, frowning. "Our love wasn't a mistake."

He ignored her. He gestured with the gun for Mia and Gracie to start up the ladder. The water was now at shin level and climbing fast. Mia took Gracie's hand, fear strong in her eyes as she helped her little girl. "It's okay, honey. I'm right behind you."

"I'm sorry, Mia," Dr. Elias said.

She turned. "But you're going to murder us anyway?" Mia's chin jutted, her voice low so Gracie would not hear.

"As I said, I'm sorry. I really mean that."

Mia gave the doctor her back and continued up to the attic. Dallas figured he had one chance to turn the tide in their favor, but he had to make sure Mia and Gracie were far enough away.

"Up, Juno," he commanded.

Juno scrambled up the ladder with the ease born of hours of training in every possible situation from planes to boats to escalators. The dog sensed no danger, only another adventure awaiting him.

He heard Gracie giggle from up in the attic. "Good job, Juno."

The tear in his heart widened. They could not die. He could not let them drown.

"Now you," Dr. Elias said, swiveling the gun not to Dallas, but to Susan.

Her mouth fell open. "What? What are you saying?"

"I'm saying," Elias said, fury kindling on his face, "that you ruined me, my career, my marriage, everything. Getting involved with you was the worst day in my life and having you show up in Spanish Canyon was the second. You're going to die along with them, Susan. You should have died a long time ago."

Horror dawned in her expression, creeping up to overtake the love that had been there a moment before. "How can you say this to me? You are the only man I've ever loved. I killed Peter Finnigan and got these people here so we could have a future."

"I never even told Peter you were in on Asa's murder. He didn't even know we hatched that little plot together. He did not have to die."

"Well, he's dead, and that can't be changed," she said. "We have to think about the future."

"We have no future. Can't you understand that?" he said, voice like the last peal of a funeral bell. "You will climb the ladder and die with the rest of them."

The color disappeared from her face. "But I love you. We have a whole life ahead of us."

"I had a future and I threw it away for money and because I thought I cared about you. After I killed your husband, you ran. And you know what? I deserved that because it showed me I never really loved you at all."

"That's not true," she protested. "You did. You did love me."

"You were a means to an end, Susan, a shortcut I never

should have taken. That's all." The words dropped like bullets.

With a cry, Susan took out a knife, the one she had stolen from Dallas's kitchen, and sprang at Dr. Elias. He deflected her, dealing a blow to the side of her head that made her cry out and fall backward, grabbing the rocking chair for support.

Dallas used the moment of distraction to launch himself at Dr. Elias.

He threw a fist, aiming for the doctor's face, but an incoming gush of water knocked him off target. His punch connected with Elias's temple, but not hard enough to do the job. Elias fired. Dallas felt a sharp trail of fire shoot through his body as he splashed backward into the water.

NINETEEN

The shot exploded through the cabin, and Mia felt as if the bullet bisected her own body. Instinctively, she shoved Gracie farther into the attic, the floor of which had been covered with plywood to provide a surface for storage.

"Dallas," she screamed, grabbing at the barking Juno to prevent him from going back down the ladder. He whined and looked from her toward his fallen master. She strained to see into the dim space. Had Dallas gone under? Had the bullet passed by him?

"He's not dead," Susan snapped. "You shot him through the shoulder. Terrible aim."

Mia's breath squeezed out in panicked bursts. He was not dead. Dallas was still alive. Her thoughts focused on that one paramount fact.

"I'm a doctor, not a sniper. Help him up the ladder, Susan," Elias commanded.

"I won't."

Juno continued to bark.

"Shut that dog up," Elias shouted, "or I'll shoot him, too. I can't think with all that racket."

Mia stroked Juno's head. "It's okay, Juno," she whispered. "Quiet now."

"Don't cry, doggie," Gracie added, petting his trembling

flanks with her tiny hands. The lamplight glinted off the gun as Dr. Elias pointed it at Susan.

"Yes, you will get him up that ladder, because if you don't, I will kill you down here, and I don't think you want to be shot, do you?"

She didn't answer.

"Do you?" he demanded, louder. "You've never liked discomfort, Susan. Always enjoyed the nice things, the easy answers. I don't think a bullet hole would suit you."

Susan splashed over to Dallas and took his arm. His groan of pain shot through Mia.

"Gently," she could not stop herself from saying.

"This is crazy," Elias said with a strangled cry. "The whole thing is insane. How did it come to this?"

"You can stop it," Mia called. "You are an excellent doctor and you've helped lots of people. Catherine said you are a good father, too."

"She said that?" His tone grew soft. "Then I didn't totally destroy everything."

Mia felt a spark of hope. "No, you haven't. You could let us go. Then you would be able to see your children, maybe. Still be a father to them."

He paused. "Thank you, Mia, for saying that, but it will be better for them if I disappear. I'm not going to withstand jail. I don't have that kind of strength. I wish things could have been different. I sincerely do."

"But…" She realized he was no longer listening. He moved aside, water splashing nearly to his waist as Susan staggered with Dallas to the ladder and they crowded up together. Mia reached out and eased Dallas as best she could into the attic space where he knelt, one hand on the wood for support, the other clutching his shoulder. Juno licked Dallas and turned in happy circles.

Mia immediately ripped off the bottom hem of her

T-shirt and wadded it up, pressing it to the profusely bleeding wound. "Dallas, I'm so sorry. I'm so, so sorry."

He looked up, gave her a tight, forced grin. "Not your fault. Is Gracie okay?"

"I'm okay," Gracie said. "Didja' get shot?" Her eyes were round as quarters in the darkening attic.

"Yeah. Forgot to duck," he said.

"Silly," she answered.

Susan stood at the attic access, staring down at Elias. "You won't get away from me," she hissed. "You will not go anywhere without me."

He laughed. "Watch me." Then he shut the trapdoor. The sound of scraping wood indicated he'd secured it from the outside.

Susan pounded on the hatch, screaming obscenities. "I knew you were a coward, Thomas. Deep down, I always knew it. That's why I went to Cora's house, to be sure you had the guts to follow through."

Mia drew Gracie away and left the woman to her rant. It was more important to figure out how they were going to escape. Dallas was considering the same thing, eyeing the nailed plywood floor.

He ran his hand over the seams. "Try to find a spot where the boards have warped or broken."

Though she didn't want to tear her attention away from Dallas, she did as he indicated.

Gracie crawled into the low spots near the walls.

Splinters drove into Mia's fingers, but she continued to search feverishly.

"I can hear the water," Gracie announced, her ear to a crack between two boards. Dallas and Mia hastened over. Gracie had found a place where one of the boards had splintered away, leaving an inch gap.

"Good work, Gracie." Dallas shoved his fingers into the gap and began pulling on the weakened board, the effort dappling his face with beads of sweat. When he'd lifted the board enough for her to get her hands in, Mia added her strength, yanking on the old wood until it gave way with a crack and a puff of dust.

"Okay," Dallas panted. "Now we can pull up the other boards."

Susan joined in and soon they had cleared enough boards away to create a small hole. Dallas lowered himself into the opening and kicked away the Sheetrock.

"There's the water," Gracie said. "I see it."

The level was only a few feet below the attic floor. Mia shuddered.

Dallas sat at the edge, feet dangling into the opening. "I'm going to swim through the house and make sure there's an exit."

"Dallas…" But he was already done, dropping down into the water after sucking in a deep breath. Juno dove in with him.

Gracie peered into the water. "When's he gonna come back, Mommy?"

Mia wrapped an arm around her girl's shoulders, holding here there to feel the reassuring rise and fall of her breathing. "Soon."

The seconds ticked into minutes.

"Do you think he drowned?" Susan said.

Mia turned on her. "Don't say that. He's doing his best to get us out of here in spite of all the damage you and Dr. Elias have done."

Susan broke into a smile. "You love him, don't you?"

Mia turned away from the crazy woman who had her own twisted version of love. Susan's infatuation had turned into an obsession, and Dr. Elias a possession that she had to acquire.

Love wasn't like that. It was an overwhelming desire to see the other person happy, healthy and thriving. She wanted that for Dallas with all the passion inside her. She wanted him to find a reason to put down roots and allow himself to have the family she knew he would treasure, with a woman who wasn't on the wrong side of the law, mother to a child of a drug lord. He deserved more than that.

Susan would never understand. Love wasn't holding on tightly. It was letting go, even when it hurt.

Dallas surfaced, sucking in a mighty breath of air. Juno popped up next to him.

"We have to get to the front door. I wedged it open. Can you do it?"

"Of course," she said, but his eyes were not on her. He was considering Gracie. He reached out a wet hand for hers, wincing only slightly, voice husky with pain.

"Hey, Goldfish girl."

Gracie giggled and took his hand. "You're wet."

"Yep. And it's time for you to get wet, too. I need you to take a big breath and hold it and we're gonna swim to the door down there. Okay?"

Gracie's mouth tightened. "I'm scared to do that."

"Juno will be there with you. You can hold on to his collar. How would that be?"

"Okay, I guess, but what if my breath won't hold in that long?"

Dallas riveted his eyes to hers. "God made you a strong lady, like your mama. You're gonna be okay and that's a promise. We'll get Goldfish after."

"The pizza-flavored kind?"

He laughed. "Any kind you want."

Gracie nodded. She sat on the edge of the plywood and stuck in her feet. "Cold, cold."

Juno paddled over and rested his paws on her lap, which set her to giggling. Dallas switched on a button that made a red light blink on Juno's collar. "Now you can see him. Ready?"

She nodded.

He turned to Mia and Susan. "Straight down and to the right. Give us a couple of minutes then follow."

He held up an open palm, and Mia grasped it, pulling strength and comfort from those long fingers. Then she helped Gracie over the edge, heart pulsing with fear as she watched the water close over her daughter's head.

I must be getting old. Dallas had been a tough guy, once. Recovered from stabbings, alcohol poisoning and even a snakebite, which had been worse than any of it, but now he felt weakened, the pain in his shoulder swelling with every arm stroke. Or maybe it was the added worry about escorting a tiny child through eight feet of water when her eyes were wide and terrified; panic beginning to set in on her face.

She clung to Juno's collar as he swam. They bobbed up, skimming the surface just under the ceiling. Gracie pressed her face so it was nearly touching the plaster, sucking in fearful breaths along with some water that set her to coughing. When they reached the far wall, he called over the surging water.

"We're going under now, Gracie. Only for a minute and then we'll be out the door.

"No, no," she said, choking on a mouthful of water. "I don't wanna."

Dallas was not confident that his calm reasoning skills were enough to counter Gracie's growing fears. What would Mia do? She hadn't yet caught up and there wasn't time. In a moment, the gap would be inundated and Gracie would be breathing in water instead of air. No time, Dallas. What are you going to do?

He flashed on how his mother had handled things when

Dallas or his brother had come home bleeding or with some sort of contusion. Quick and efficient, before there was too much time for fear to bloom.

He took Gracie around the shoulders. "All right. Deep breath with me. Ready? Go!" Dallas heaved in a breath in exaggerated fashion and Gracie did the same. Then he pulled her underwater and dove for the door.

It was slow going with one good arm and Gracie wiggling in terror, pressing on his bullet wound. Juno managed the dive ahead of them, and Dallas followed in the dog's wake. He could make out nothing but the red blinking light on Juno's collar.

Gracie's movements became more frantic.

Don't breathe in, he wanted to say.

She grabbed at his neck, then started to push away.

Time was up. She would be sucking in water in a matter of seconds.

He tightened his hold on her and made for the door, kicking as hard as he dared.

They surged through and rocketed out the other side. He propelled them both to the surface and nearly brained himself on the roof gutter which was inches from the crown of his head. He grabbed the edge with one hand and held Gracie's head above water with the other.

For the longest moment of his life, she didn't make a sound.

Terror balled in his stomach and shot through his nerves. "Gracie," he shouted, giving her a shake.

Her head came up and she started coughing, vomiting up mouthfuls of water in between anguished cries. It was the sweetest sound he'd ever heard.

"Good girl, Gracie. You did great. The scary stuff is over now."

She cried and clung to his neck. "I don't wanna do that again."

He laughed. "Me, neither. I'm going to put you up on the roof now and go get your mama."

She shook her head. "No, I don't want to."

"I heard you could climb up a tree." He gave her a sideways look. "But maybe I remembered that wrong."

"I can climb a tree," she insisted, indignation stiffening her chin.

"Let's see then. Pretend I'm a tree. Climb up on my shoulders and onto the roof."

She did, setting darts of agony zipping through his wound. She got up on the roof and crouched into a little ball. "It's scary up here. I don't want to stay."

"It will just be for a minute, and then your mommy will come."

Dallas removed the blinking collar light and wrangled Juno out of the water and onto the roof. The dog immediately sat down next to Gracie and licked her all over.

"Be right back." He sank back down in the water, hanging the red light to a nail that stuck out of the doorframe. He felt, rather than saw, the two women kicking their way down. He grabbed an arm, Susan's or Mia's he was not sure and dragged that person toward the door before he did the same for the other, orienting himself using the red light. For the second time he emerged, physically spent, just under the eaves of the submerged cabin. It was all he could do to catch his breath.

"Gracie," Mia cried, scanning frantically, as she broke the surface.

He pointed upward, still gasping.

Craning her neck, she must have caught sight of her daughter. Tears began to stream down her face and she closed the distance between them, and kissed all the pain from his body.

Mia was not sure how they would escape from the rooftop, but she simply could not bring her mind to fret about it much. Gracie was there, safe and sound, her skinny knees tucked under her as she threw pine needles into the water below. Juno kept a watchful eye on her. Susan and Dallas scrambled to the peak of the roof.

"There he is," Susan said.

Mia blinked out of her euphoric trance. "Dr. Elias?"

"Out in the lake," Dallas grunted. "Must have had motor trouble because he's rowing."

"He never was much of a sailor," Susan said with disgust.

Dallas peered into the darkness. "After all this. Can't believe he got away."

Susan continued to watch Dr. Elias make his escape. "We could have been together forever."

Mia noted the revulsion that bubbled in Dallas's eyes. "The police will arrest him," he grumbled. "I'll get my phone."

Susan removed a plastic bag with a phone inside.

"No need," she said, voice soft, fingers pressing the buttons. "I knew he was angry with me so I planned ahead." She sighed. "Of course, I thought he would see reason. I thought I could convince him we were meant to be together."

Mia flashed back to Peter Finnigan. "What do you mean you planned ahead?"

Dallas must have come to the same conclusion because he and Mia both lunged for Susan at the same moment. Too late. With a moonlit smile on her dreamy face, she pressed the last button. There was a deafening blast from out on the lake, and Dr. Elias's boat exploded into a shower of golden sparks.

TWENTY

"What was that?" Gracie said, standing up so quickly she nearly toppled off the roof.

Mia closed her mouth, and Dallas was once again amazed at the strength of mothers to make every circumstance all right for their children. "It was a little explosion. It's not going to hurt us."

He could not comprehend Susan, the woman who had just blown up the man she purported to love, the man for whom she had committed multiple murders. Love and murder. How could they go together? There was not much time to mull it over as two Zodiac boats roared up to the flooded cabin.

Mia waved frantically, and he would have helped if his shoulder hadn't been useless. As it was, he struggled to keep upright against the dizziness.

In a moment, one boat had peeled off toward the burning wreckage. The other was captained by Detective Stiving, who grabbed Antonia's arm and forced her to sit.

"You're going to fall out," he snapped.

Antonia stood again anyway and screamed. "Mia, are you all right? Do you have Gracie?"

Mia was crying so hard she could not choke out a response.

"Yes," Dallas called down. "Mia and Gracie are fine. Susan is here, too. She just blew up Dr. Elias's boat."

Stiving held up a pair of handcuffs. "We're ready for her."

With an elaborate combination of coaxing and lifting, Gracie, Mia, Susan and Juno were loaded into the Zodiac. Stiving wasted no time cuffing Susan. Dallas contemplated his useless arm. "I'm gonna jump," he said. "Too hard to climb down."

Stiving shook his head. "You always were a nutcase."

With that endorsement ringing in his ears, Dallas plunged feet first into the frigid water. When he surfaced, Mia and Antonia dragged him into the boat where he collapsed.

Mia pulled a blanket around him.

He tried to protest. "You need it."

She ignored him and opened Stiving's first-aid kit. Antonia sat with Gracie held tight in her arms, crooning some soft endearments meant for the child's ears only.

Susan sat in silence, staring out toward the ruined boat.

Stiving flicked a glance at Dallas. "Took one in the shoulder, huh? Not so agile as you pretend to be."

"Apparently not." He bit back a groan as Mia pressed a cloth to his shoulder. "And you're not as thick-headed as you pretend to be, Stiving. Did Antonia finally convince you we were telling the truth?"

He grinned. "Nah. Actually I did some research, called some colleagues and interviewed Catherine Elias. I even discovered that Susan's poor, drowned husband was a demolitions expert and his wife worked for the company. Interesting, don't you think?"

"It explains her prowess in blowing people up."

"So you see, I really am a good cop after all."

"*Good* is a relative term."

Stiving laughed. "Just be quiet and we'll get you to a hospital, Black."

He did remain silent for a while, the pulsing of the engine shuddering through him. Mia adjusted the blanket, fiddled with the bandages, and mopped his face all the way back to the landing spot where Susan was transferred to Stiving's police car. Gracie, bundled to the ears, was loaded into another official vehicle driven by a volunteer who gave Juno a skeptical look.

"Do I have to take him, too? His paws are muddy."

Juno responded with a massive shake that sprayed the volunteer with water from head to boots.

Gracie laughed. "Come on, Juno. Get out of the cold, quick before you catch germans."

Juno leapt into the car and settled himself on the backseat as the dripping volunteer grumbled his way to the driver's door.

"There's a National Guard rescue crew coming, but they'll be another few minutes," Stiving said. "Most direct routes here are flooded." He raised an eyebrow. "You aren't going to bleed out or anything are you? That would create way too much paperwork for me."

"I'll try to spare you that."

Stiving nodded and went to speak to the captain of the other Zodiac, leaving Dallas propped on a plastic tarp, his back to a boulder, Mia kneeling next to him. She wasn't crying, but her brown eyes were bright, water droplets glittering in her curling strands of hair.

"I can't say the words," she said, taking his hands in hers. "How can I tell you how incredibly thankful I am?"

His heart lurched inside. She was so beautiful, bedraggled, exhausted, bruised and utterly, incomparably beautiful. "We did it together," he managed.

She shook her head. "I've been trying so hard to fashion some sort of life for myself and you know what? I figured out that I already have one."

He stroked the satin of her cheek.

He heard her choke back a sound, the sort of vulnerable tiny peep that a chick might make when confronted with the edge of the nest.

"My whole life," she continued, "is Gracie and…" She stopped, looked away.

Dallas, the man who had never been able to decipher the first thing about women, wondered. Could the tenderness he saw in her face match the love buried deep in his own heart that swelled and undulated like the flood? He took her hand and cleared his throat. Fish or cut bait. Take the chance, or let his heart fly away to Florida. "You and Gracie…" He sucked in a breath and started again. "I hoped that it might be you and Gracie and me."

She jerked, mouth open.

Had he blown it? Scared her right into flight? Misunderstood a woman as he had countless times before? *Do it. Say it,* something deep inside him urged. "Mia, I'm not traditional father material, and you are an amazing mother who doesn't need any help parenting, but all my life I've been waiting for a partner to put down roots with."

She blinked, staring at him.

"You want roots?"

He sighed. *If you're going to bury yourself, might as well go all the way.* "No. I want you. And Gracie. And the life I know we could have together."

Silence.

"I've done bad things, Mia, things I can't sponge away or keep hidden, not from you. You know the good and bad of me and if you feel at all like you could love me, I would like to build a life with you and Gracie." He said it louder than he'd meant to. "I love you."

She gripped his hands. "But I've been to jail."

"Me, too."

"My ex-husband was a drug dealer."

"I know."

"I have control issues and a stubborn daughter and I eat too many sweets and I have terrible handwriting."

"I love you."

Her expression remained frozen somewhere between amusement and something unidentifiable. Fear? Love?

"Dallas, I'm not sure what to say."

"Say we can build a family together as slowly as you need it to happen. I'm not good at following rules, I don't know how to make mac and cheese and I spend most of my time with a dog. But I'm patient. I've got that going for me."

She smiled, lighting a fire in his belly. "Say you love me, too," he choked out.

She leaned closed and stopped, her mouth a tantalizing half inch from his. "I love you, too, Dallas."

Then there was warmth where he was cold, relief for his pain, and the sun triumphing over the floodwaters of his soul as he gathered her close.

Over the crush of joy, he became aware of a high-pitched noise, the squeals and laughter of Antonia and Gracie as they watched the proceedings from the car window. Juno added a robust bark.

He smiled and kissed her again.

Mia turned her face to the sun, relishing the warmth that drove away the last remnants of the storm some two weeks after Gracie's rescue. Spanish Canyon and the entire county was an official disaster area according to the federal government. Efforts were underway for a massive cleanup. Mia was ready to begin her own restoration project.

Dallas looped his good arm around her shoulders and planted a kiss on the top of her head as they stared at the burned wreckage of Cora's house. Gracie poked a stick into the various mudholes she was able to locate with Juno sniffing right along behind. "You sure you want to tackle this?" he said, gesturing to the ruined structure.

She snuggled into his side, careful not to put too much pressure on his shoulder. "I think Cora would have been pleased to see another house built here on the property she loved so much."

"And the matchmaker in her would have appreciated the fact that we're doing this together."

"For our future." Ours. The thought thrilled through her like the spring breeze. If all went well, the house would be built and the beautiful flower beds restored in time for their fall wedding. Closing her eyes, Mia could imagine the details. Gracie with her little basket of flowers, probably followed closely by a four-legged, hairy attendant. Antonia and Reuben would be there to add their heartfelt blessings along with Dallas's friends from the Search and Rescue school where he had signed on to work indefinitely.

"Still," Mia said, an ache in her throat. "I wish Cora was here to see it."

"She'll see it," Dallas said. "And she'll have the best view of all."

"Dallas," she said, turning to face him and marveling once again at the strength and gentleness she saw there. "This place was where I lost my dear friend. I thought I'd never come back."

"And?"

"And now it's the place where I am going to start my life over again. Pain and joy, all in one place."

"Blessings are like that, I think."

She kissed him, pressing him close, her future husband and irreplaceable blessing.

"Hiya," Gracie said, coming over with her muddy stick. "I'm hungry."

Mia laughed. "You're always hungry."

Dallas retrieved a package from the stash in his truck.

He handed the pizza-flavored Goldfish crackers to Gracie. "Don't feed too many to Juno," he said, voice stern but eyes twinkling.

"Okay," Gracie agreed.

"And don't fill up before lunch," Dallas said, taking one more item from the truck. He shook the blue box. "We'll go back to the trailer you and your mom rented and I'm going to cook up some mac and cheese. This time, I'm following the directions."

"Hooray," Gracie squealed and Juno barked along with her. "But just in case, can Mommy help?"

Mia and Dallas laughed as Gracie raced off to chase a pair of butterflies.

"I dunno, Mr. Black," Mia teased. "Rebuilding a house is one thing, but tackling mac and cheese?"

"Don't worry," Dallas said, sliding his arms around her again. "Even an old dog can learn new tricks."

"That's what they say." She kissed him. "But I think I'll stick around to help."

His eyes reflected the light as the sun broke through the clouds. "I wouldn't have it any other way."

* * * * *

Dear Reader,

Floods, fires, famines, earthquakes! We live in a violent world prone to catastrophes. In this last book in the Storm-swept series, Mia and Dallas must navigate floodwaters and the torrent of violence that follows in the wake of a decades-old crime. In real life, no matter what type of environment we live in, we're all prone to dangers both external and spiritual. The only life preserver we can hang on to is our loving God who is our safety in the storm and our guarantee of salvation.

Friends, I hope you are swept along in the story and, as always, I am blessed that you spent some of your precious time reading my book. Feel free to contact me via my website at www.danamentink.com if you'd like to chat. There is also a physical address there if you prefer to correspond by letter.

God bless,

Dana Mentink

Questions for Discussion

1. Mia and Dallas both struggle with their previous choices. Is it possible to escape a difficult past? What advice can you offer someone who is crippled by past situations?

2. Dallas and Juno have a unique bond that surpasses dog/owner. Have you experienced such a bond with an animal? Explain.

3. Dallas and Mia are both hampered by fear in different ways. How does it impact their life choices?

4. Dallas has disrespect for rules. Do you know anyone like that? Describe them.

5. What kind of mother is Mia Sandoval?

6. Do you think Hector Sandoval has really repented? How is it possible to tell if a person's repentance is sincere or a form of manipulation?

7. What was Dallas's motivation for getting into gang life? Why do you think he stayed in it, in spite of his brother's efforts to extricate him?

8. What is behind Dallas's "restless urge to move on"?

9. Why do we so desperately cling to our own plans, even when they appear to crumble around us? Is there a better way?

10. Do you think Antonia did the right thing by hiring

Dallas to keep watch over Mia without her knowledge? Why or why not?

11. Gracie believes her daddy is a bad man. How would you describe Hector Sandoval's actions to his young daughter?

12. What spiritual battles do believers fight on a daily basis?

13. Why is it so hard to do things on our own? What does God have to say about this?

14. Mia is afraid to trust her choices and her judgments. Have you ever felt this way? What is the antidote for that fear?

15. What do you imagine the future holds for Mia, Dallas and Gracie?

REQUEST YOUR FREE BOOKS!

2 FREE RIVETING INSPIRATIONAL NOVELS
PLUS 2 FREE MYSTERY GIFTS

YES! Please send me 2 FREE Love Inspired® Suspense novels and my 2 FREE mystery gifts (gifts are worth about $10). After receiving them, if I don't wish to receive any more books, I can return the shipping statement marked "cancel." If I don't cancel, I will receive 4 brand-new novels every month and be billed just $4.74 per book in the U.S. or $5.24 per book in Canada. That's a savings of at least 21% off the cover price. It's quite a bargain! Shipping and handling is just 50¢ per book in the U.S. and 75¢ per book in Canada.* I understand that accepting the 2 free books and gifts places me under no obligation to buy anything. I can always return a shipment and cancel at any time. Even if I never buy another book, the two free books and gifts are mine to keep forever.

123/323 IDN F5AC

Name _____ (PLEASE PRINT) _____

Address _____ Apt. # _____

City _____ State/Prov. _____ Zip/Postal Code _____

Signature (if under 18, a parent or guardian must sign)

Mail to the Harlequin® Reader Service:
IN U.S.A.: P.O. Box 1867, Buffalo, NY 14240-1867
IN CANADA: P.O. Box 609, Fort Erie, Ontario L2A 5X3

**Are you a current subscriber to Love Inspired Suspense books
and want to receive the larger-print edition?
Call 1-800-873-8635 or visit www.ReaderService.com.**

* Terms and prices subject to change without notice. Prices do not include applicable taxes. Sales tax applicable in N.Y. Canadian residents will be charged applicable taxes. Offer not valid in Quebec. This offer is limited to one order per household. Not valid for current subscribers to Love Inspired Suspense books. All orders subject to credit approval. Credit or debit balances in a customer's account(s) may be offset by any other outstanding balance owed by or to the customer. Please allow 4 to 6 weeks for delivery. Offer available while quantities last.

Your Privacy—The Harlequin® Reader Service is committed to protecting your privacy. Our Privacy Policy is available online at www.ReaderService.com or upon request from the Harlequin Reader Service.
We make a portion of our mailing list available to reputable third parties that offer products we believe may interest you. If you prefer that we not exchange your name with third parties, or if you wish to clarify or modify your communication preferences, please visit us at www.ReaderService.com/consumerschoice or write to us at Harlequin Reader Service Preference Service, P.O. Box 9062, Buffalo, NY 14269. Include your complete name and address.

"We used to count the stars at night, Jack. Remember that?"

Oh, he remembered, all right. They'd look skyward and watch each star appear, summer, winter, spring and fall, each season offering its own array, a blend of favorites. Until they'd become distracted by other things. Sweet things.

A sigh welled from somewhere deep within him, a quiet blooming of what could have been. "I remember."

They stared upward, side by side, watching the sunset fade to streaks of lilac and gray. Town lights began to appear north of the bridge, winking on earlier now that it was August. "How long are you here?"

Olivia faltered. "I'm not sure."

He turned to face her, puzzled.

"I'm between lives right now."

He raised an eyebrow, waiting for her to continue. She did, after drawn-out seconds, but didn't look at him. She kept her gaze up and out, watching the tree shadows darken and dim.

"I was married."

He'd heard she'd gotten married several years ago, but the "was" surprised him. He dropped his gaze to her left hand. No ring. No tan line that said a ring had been there this summer. A flicker that might be hope stirred in his chest, but entertaining those notions would get him nothing but trouble, so he blamed the strange feeling on the half-finished sandwich he'd wolfed down on the drive in.

You've eaten fast plenty of times before this and been fine. Just fine.

The reminder made him take a half step forward, just close enough to inhale the scent of sweet vanilla on her hair, her skin.

He shouldn't. He knew that. He knew it even as his hand reached for her hand, the left one bearing no man's ring, and that touch, the press of his fingers on hers, made the tiny flicker inside brighten just a little.

The surroundings, the trees, the thin-lit night and the sound of rushing water made him feel as if anything was possible, and he hadn't felt that way in a very long time. But here, with her?

He did. And it felt good

Find out what else is going on in Jasper Gulch in
HIS MONTANA SWEETHEART by Ruth Logan Herne,
available August 2014 from Love Inspired®.

Love Inspired
SUSPENSE
RIVETING INSPIRATIONAL ROMANCE

Emma Landers has amnesia. Problem is, she can't remember how she got it, why she's injured or why someone wants to hurt her. When she lands on the doorstep of former love Travis Wright, she can barely remember their past history. But she knows she can trust him to protect her. The handsome farmer was heartbroken when Emma left him for the big city. But there's no way he can send her away when gunshots start flying. Now Travis must keep Emma safe while helping her piece together her memories—before it's too late.

A TRACE OF MEMORY
by
VALERIE HANSEN

THE DEFENDERS

Protecting children in need

Available August 2014 wherever
Love Inspired books and ebooks are sold.

LI44613